虞学泽 著
童孝华 译

水质时光

The Water-Like Time

中央编译出版社
Central Compilation & Translation Press

Preface

It was not until the yellow leaves fell that my poems emerged in large numbers. After all, writing poems is just a hobby of mine, and I never thought I would have to show them to the public one day.

Over the past forty years since boyhood, I have been reading and writing poems, growing, accumulating foundations, and slowly enriching my gorgeous and thin words with my life and my view of the world. I used to be wild in filling my heart and life with poetry, but I also used to neglect poetry on the pretext of mundane matters. But one thing has remained the same: no matter life is bright or dark, a candle light with a poetic wick is always on in the bottom of my heart.

So the moment of happiness and sorrow encountered in life and the flowery fire of life have naturally poured out in the same language.

Yes, write them down. Write them all down.

How many people are striving for their own

自 序

直到黄叶飘落,我的诗们才蜂攒蚁集。但我还是暗暗有些惶恐,毕竟写诗只是我的心头好而已,从未想过有朝一日要拿它们"示众"。

从青涩少年算起,四十年来,我不断地读诗,写诗,成长,积淀,慢慢地以我的人生和对世界的看法来丰富从前华丽却单薄的词藻。我曾经疯狂地用诗歌填满我全部的心胸和生活,也曾以俗事缠身等种种借口来冷落诗歌。但有一点却始终未变:无论生活或明或暗,一豆诗芯烛灯时刻在我的心底亮着。

于是,生活中遇到的片刻喜忧,生命中感悟的点滴花火,便自然而然地以同一种语言倾泄而出。

是的,写下来。把它们都写下来。

多少人在孜孜以求各自的幸福,但是人生仅有幸

happiness, but life is not enough just to have happiness. Richness is much thicker and broader than happiness, and richness means more than happiness.

Why has classical music become a classic through the centuries? It's because it has infinite richness. Why does the same Chopin's *Fantaisie—Impromptu* sound like sunflowers in the sun for some, autumn leaves drifting in unpredictable life for others, and nostalgia for the country for still others? This is because of richness.

Where does the richness come from? It comes partly from the experience in life. I myself have been a worker, farmer, soldier, student, and businessman, but personal experience is ultimately limited, and reading and writing make me richer.

Reading is to face the authors and listen to them, so that you can appreciate more people's lives in your life, thus enriching your world infinitely. Writing, on the other hand, is to face yourself faithfully, talk with yourself, dig into your own hidden realm, and thus discover more of yourself in a different way.

I started writing poetry when I was less than twenty years old, and over the past forty years, no matter what industry I was in or what position I held, in addition to keeping up with my reading, I have always written poetry, and I have made many poet friends. Why do I write?

福是不够的。丰富要比幸福厚重得多,宽广得多,丰富的意义要超越幸福。

为什么古典音乐历经几百年能够成为经典?就是因为它具有无限的丰富性。为什么同一首肖邦的《即兴幻想曲》,有人听出了阳光下的向日葵,有人听出了秋叶飘零人生无常,有人则听出了去国怀乡?这就是丰富性。

丰富来自哪里?人生的阅历是一面,从我自己讲,工农兵学商都经历了,但是个人的体验终究是有限的,更丰富的一面仍是阅读与写作。

阅读是面对作者、倾听别人,让自己的一生能够领略更多人的人生,从而无限地丰富自己的世界。写作则是忠实地面对自己,与自己对话,挖掘自己的隐秘之境,从而发现更多不同的自己。

我在不到二十岁的时候就开始写诗,四十年来,不管在什么行业,在什么职位,除了保持阅读,一直笔耕不辍,也交了很多诗友。为什么写?一方面确实有很

One is that I really have a lot of feelings, emotions and thoughts to express to myself, and one is that the world is full of things, so I must leave a space for myself to be alone, to cleanse my mind from time to time, and often to bathe in new thinking and moving. In this process, there will be countless unfamiliar me jumping out to surprise and amaze myself.

Many of the poems in this collection are also about my hometown; they are a dialogue between my hometown and me. In fact, I left home when I was young, and my path in life does not entirely belong to my geographical hometown. In many cases, I was a man on the way, just as *Laozi Is on the Way*, a book I wrote. However, I have a greater affection for my hometown than others. In the days far and near from my hometown, poems have never left me, or rather I have never left them. They are the only thing that keep my heart beating close to the pulse of my hometown and keep my life in a balanced upward and resistant posture to this day.

The times have been so turbulent that the title of poet has fallen out of prosperity and poetry has become a luxury. I remember that Professor Zhou Fucheng of Peking University still swore to the world in his twilight years: "This time, I am learning to cry and to laugh, but I am not learning well. I envy Shakespeare's laugh at

多的感触、情绪和思想要向自己倾诉宣泄；另一方面，世事纷杂，一定要留一个空间让自己独处，时时荡涤蒙垢的心灵，常常沐浴新的思维与感动。在这个过程中，就会有无数个陌生的我跳将出来让自己惊喜和惊叹。

这本诗集中的作品也有许多是关于故乡的，是我与故乡的对话。事实上，我少小离家，我的人生之路，并不完全属于地理上的故乡。在许多时候，我是一个在路上的人，正如我的《老子在路上》。但我对故乡的感情，却更甚于他人。在与故乡远远近近的日子里，诗一直没有离开过我，或者说我一直未曾离开过它。唯有它，让我的心跳始终与故乡的脉搏紧紧地连在一起，并且让我的人生至今仍保持着一种均衡向上和抗争的姿态。

时代风起云涌，诗人的称号已繁华落尽，诗歌成了奢侈品。记得北京大学周辅成教授到了暮年依旧向世人宣誓："这时候，我在学哭，也在学笑。但哭笑都学得不好。我羡慕莎士比亚对福斯塔夫的笑，羡慕达·芬

Falstaff, I envy Leonardo da Vinci's *Mona Lisa's* laugh at good and evil, and I long for Tolstoy's crying after listening to Tchaikovsky's *Song of the Andes* and reading France's Boétie's *The Discourse of Voluntary Servitude*, but I can't learn how. But I still have to cry and laugh."

I think, no matter when, I will "keep crying and laughing" and continue writing poems, so that my life will always be true and rich.

This is the preface.

Yu Xueze

Shanghai

December 9, 2019

奇所画的《蒙娜丽莎》超善恶的笑,同时也向往托尔斯泰听完柴可夫斯基的《如歌的行板》和读完法国波埃西《自愿奴役论》后的哭。但我要学他们怎么也学不到。不过我仍要哭笑。"

我想,无论到什么时候,我也"仍要哭笑",仍要写诗,让自己的人生永葆那一份真和丰富。

是为序。

虞学泽

2019年12月9日于上海

CONTENTS

002 / The Water—Like Time

004 / That's a Black—Topped Boat

012 / I Am at One End and You at the Other

016 / Persistence

022 / Pedestrian Street in Summer

026 / Moonlight on the Huansha River

030 / The Morning Sun of the Xixiao River

034 / Twilight in Lu Xun's Hometown

040 / Echoes of South Second Beltway of Shaoxing

046 / Street Lamp at the NO.1 Water Street in Shaoxing

048 / The Silk Shop at Noon

052 / Meditation on the Celebrity Square

058 / Morning in An Alley

064 / The Poetic Soul of the Grand Canal

068 / Record

072 / Goose Pond

目　录

水质时光……………………………003

就是那只乌篷船……………………005

我在这头　你在那头………………013

执着…………………………………017

夏天的步行街………………………023

浣纱江的月光………………………027

晨曦…………………………………031

黄昏…………………………………035

回声…………………………………041

路灯…………………………………047

正午时的丝绸屋……………………049

沉思…………………………………053

小巷的早晨…………………………059

大运河的诗魂………………………065

记载…………………………………069

鹅池…………………………………073

076 / Seeing the Puyang River Again

080 / We Still Have an Appointment
084 / We Were Separated Only by the Distance between Desks
094 / A Salute to Teachers
100 / Thou
104 / Ode to Comrades in Arms
116 / A Reunion of Veterans
122 / Revisit Yang Village
132 / I'm Proud of My Youth
140 / Your Silhouette in Charging
146 / Salute! I Do Not Want to Disturb You
150 / The Moon Is a Faint Nostalgia
154 / Everlasting Nostalgia

162 / Mother's Hands
166 / Don't Leave Me More With Memories
170 / Seeking Dreams
174 / Father's Feet
178 / Yearning
182 / Father's River
184 / My Daughter Is Wearing a Doctoral Mortarboard

又见浦阳江……………………077

我们还有约定……………………081
我们,只有课桌间的距离……………085
向老师敬礼……………………095
你……………………………101
战友颂…………………………105
老兵聚会………………………117
再回杨村………………………123
为青春骄傲……………………133
奔跑的背影……………………141
敬礼!我不惊扰你………………147
月亮是淡淡的乡愁………………151
永远的乡愁……………………155

母亲的手………………………163
不要留给我更多的回忆……………167
寻梦……………………………171
父亲的双脚……………………175
向往……………………………179
父亲的江………………………183
女儿戴上了博士帽………………185

186 / It Sounds as if My Daughter Is Calling Me

188 / The Unknown

192 / The Days of Fantasy

196 / Childhood

198 / You Are Like a Bright Star

206 / Spring

208 / Spring Snow

210 / Beginning of Spring

212 / Spring Is Approaching

214 / Late Autumn

218 / Night in Late Autumn

222 / The Autumn Color

226 / Sense of Autumn

230 / Autumn Song

232 / The Autumn Wind Brings Mid—Autumn

236 / New Year's Eve

240 / Winter Morning

244 / Snowy Night

246 / Rainy Night in Early Winter

252 / Looking Up at the Starry Sky

256 / Best Time in Life

仿佛是女儿在叫我 187
不知道 189
幻想的日子 193
童年 197
你是一颗璀璨的星 199

春 207
春雪 209
立春 211
春，来了 213
深秋 215
深秋的夜 219
秋色 223
秋意 227
秋歌 231
秋风吹来了中秋 233
年关 237
冬之晨 241
雪夜 245
初冬的雨夜 247

仰望星空 253
人生好时光 257

260 / This Night Is So Bustling

264 / Smile, Like the Blooming and Heading of the Grain

266 / A Farewell to Brussels

272 / You Are My Window

276 / The Bright Red Flag

284 / Herpes' Pain

288 / Don't Crush My Dream

292 / Delaying

296 / The Circulatory Wish

300 / Thinking of You at the Dead of Night

304 / It's Dusk Again

这个晚上真吵……………………………261
微笑,像禾谷的扬花抽穗……………265
再见!布鲁塞尔………………………267
你是我的窗……………………………273
鲜红的旗帜……………………………277
疤疹之痛………………………………285
别碾碎我的梦境………………………289
延误……………………………………293
循环的愿望……………………………297
在夜深人静时想你……………………301
又是黄昏………………………………305

The Water-Like Time

With the passing of the years,

Is there anyone who does not need to go backwards?

Hesitating on the north bank of the Hai River,

Wandering on the south bank of Hangzhou Bay,

Turning around at the estuaty of a big river into the sea,

Nothing is taken away.

In the first half of my life, I have been moving with rippled waves;

This first half of my life is the water—like time.

Looking back, the waves are the punctuations in the water;

Looking afar, the blandness is the rhythm of life.

Every difficult drift,

Is only a journey of the waves.

Every turn of time,

Is all the past that has gone with the waves.

Only my own strong chest,

And a pair of warm palms,

Remains on the paper of memory forever.

The wet marks on it are vivid,

Like the frosty flowers.

水质时光

岁月流逝
有谁不需要逆行
犹豫在海河北畔
彷徨在杭州湾南岸
转身在一条大江的入海口
什么也没有带走
我这半生啊,一直在声浪中转移
我这半生啊,是水质的时光

回眸,浪花是水中的标点
远眺,平淡是生活的节律
每一次艰难的漂流
仅仅是一段旅程的波澜
每一个光阴的转角
都是随波而去的曾经
只有自己坚实的胸膛
还有那一双温暖的手掌
永恒留在记忆的素笺上
上面的湿痕是鲜活的
像缀满的霜华

That's a Black-Topped Boat

As if it was last night's dream,
Quietly
I come back to my hometown.
The sound of oars,
The flowing water,
The black-topped boat carries you and me,
From the East Lake to the Jian Lake,
From the Luzhen to the Shen Garden.

That's a black-topped boat,
Sailing under the Bazi Bridge,
In front of the Jiezhu Temple,
At the Qingteng Book House,
At the Zhou Family Compound,
At the ancient towpath,
Sailed by Grandpa,
Sailed by Dad.

That's a black-topped boat,

就是那只乌篷船

仿佛是昨夜的梦
悄悄地
我又回到故乡
桨声欸乃
流水悠悠
乌篷船载着你载着我
从东湖到鉴湖
从鲁镇到沈园

就是那只乌篷船
在八字桥下划过
在戒珠寺前划过
在青藤书屋划过
在周家台门划过
在古纤道旁划过
爷爷划过
爸爸划过

就是那只乌篷船

Sailing in the the poems of Wen Tingyun,

In the ci poems by Lu You,

In Zhou Zuoren's writing,

In *The True Story of Ah Q*,

In the texts of elementary school.

You have read it,

So have I.

That's a black-topped boat,

Sailing in your memory,

And in my memory.

Thinking of Yu the Great passing his house three times and never entering,

Thinking of Goujian sleeping on sticks and tasting gall for his country,

Thinking of the winding stream party,

Thinking of pink hands, soft and fine, reflected in golden drops of wine,

Thinking of the word "early" in the Sanwei Study,

Thinking of the purple mulberries in the Baicao Garden,

Thinking of the two trees in the autumn night,

One was a jujube tree,

The other was also a jujube tree.

在温庭筠的诗里划过
在陆游的词里划过
在周作人笔下划过
在《阿Q正传》里划过
在小学课文里划过
你读过
我也读过

就是那只乌篷船
在你的记忆里划过
在我的记忆里划过
想起三过家门而不入
想起卧薪尝胆兴邦复国
想起曲水流觞
想起红酥手黄縢酒
想起三味书屋的那个"早"字
想起百草园里紫红的桑葚
想起秋夜里那两棵树
一棵是枣树
另一棵也是枣树

Thinking of pounding rice cakes,

Thinking of wearing new clothes,

Thinking of the sacrificial red candles in the ritual hall for ancestors,

Thinking of riding on the shoulders of adults watching the opera,

Thinking of the sound of mallets washing clothes at the river pier,

Thinking of the blush on faces after drinking liquor.

That's a black-topped boat,

Sailing on the shoulder of the sun,

Sailing with the moon's arm.

Like a man,

It toils endlessly;

Like a maiden,

Singing in the water night after night;

Like the rose,

Greeting passers-by day after day;

Like a silk thread,

Stringing one pearl after another;

Like a loving mother,

Warming the hearts of the homesick persons.

想起搡年糕

想起穿新衣

想起满堂红烛祭祖宗

想起骑在大人肩头看社戏

想起河埠头洗衣的棒槌声

想起老酒灌溉后脸上的红晕

就是那只乌篷船

搭着太阳的肩膀划过

挽着月亮的手臂划过

像汉子

生生不息地劳作

像少女

夜夜在水里唱歌

像蔷薇

天天向路人问候

像丝线

串起明珠一颗又一颗

像慈母

温暖着乡愁者的心窝

That's a black—topped boat,

Sailing in front of your door,

Sailing in front of my door.

You are missing,

You are pondering,

I'm thinking,

I'm chanting.

You should guess what I'm chanting,

I'll guess what you're thinking.

The people living by rivers and lakes enjoy their unique wisdom,

The people living by rivers and lakes enjoy their unique character.

...

就是那只乌篷船

在你的门前划过

在我的门前划过

你在想念

你在思索

我在想念

我在吟哦

你该猜到我在吟些什么

我会猜到你在想些什么

水乡人有水乡人的智慧

水乡人有水乡人的性格

……

I Am at One End and You at the Other

Having travelled for so long,
We have failed to move beyond the watery South of
 Yangtze River.
For the forests in the south of the city,
I am at one end
And you are at the other.

Still in the misty rain,
The autumn breeze comes again.
In the cups and glasses, there are the beautiful Kuaiji
 Mountain.
I am at one end
And you are at the other.

Time stretches like a shadow play,
Sitting firmly in a pot of old wine.
Watching the growth of a drop of ink on a piece of rice
 paper,
I am at one end

我在这头　你在那头

走了那么久
走不出水色江南
城南的草木
我在这头
你在那头

还在烟雨里
秋风又来
杯盏里有会稽山山清水秀
我在这头
你在那头

光阴伸缩像皮影戏
在一壶老酒里坐定
看一张宣纸上一滴墨的成长
我在这头

And you are at the other.

The Huangpu River moves like a stave,

Daling Harbor move like notes.

Whose heart is a song that resounds in the clouds?

I am at one end

And you are at the other.

Who is setting off at this moment?

Defying all the excuses,

Arriving at an exit.

I am at one end

And you are at the other.

你在那头

黄浦江涌动着五线谱
达令港起伏着音符
谁的心事是歌声响遏行云
我在这头
你在那头

此刻谁在出发
穿越所有的借口
在一个出口抵达
我在这头
你在那头

Persistence

The whole summer saw continuous high temperatures.
Driving on the Shanghai—Kunming and Changshu—Taizhou
  expressways.
Every late night, every early morning,
Every sunburn, every rainstorm.

The expressways became deep and wild.
The Jiaxing—Shaoxing Sea Bridge is full of changes,
With twinkling lights and the spilling gulls,
Emitting a dazzling aura.

Like a white flame,
Rising on the other side of the river,
Rising with the night and sleeping with the moon,
Rich, bleak, soft and beautiful.

I was driving, I was dashing,
My heart was beating noticeably faster.
I took off a pair of gentlemanly leather shoes,

执 着

整个夏天,持续高温
奔波于沪昆与常台高速
每一次深夜,每一个清晨
每一回酷晒,每一场暴雨

高速路变得深邃而旷野
嘉绍大桥充满着变幻
灯光闪烁伴着野鸥的歌鸣
放射出耀眼的光环

似白色的火焰
升腾于江的那一边
与夜色同起,与月儿同眠
丰盈、苍凉、柔美

我在行驶,我在飞奔
我的心跳明显加速
脱下装着斯文的皮鞋

But failed to remove the heaviness on my feet.

I felt as if I collided with a nail,
It turned out to be a mosquito, applying for jobs everywhere.
Found a job, passionate about serving
The firm and fresh calf belly.

I was called to wake me up.
I could not easily take off my costumes,
Facing reality, I need protection,
Continue to be dressed in decent clothes.

I would have needed nothing more,
Just wanting to revel in this shining moment.
Let go off the unconscionable loss of soul,
Slowly, slowly moving with the scenery along the way.

There is no perfect form of life.
Drinking a cup of tea, eating a meal,
Reading a good book and listening to an old song,
Let go off selfish and ancient mediocrity.

脱不掉脚上的沉重

仿佛碰撞了一枚钉子
原来是一只蚊子,到处应聘
找到了打工岗位,热情服务于
小腿肚的结实而鲜嫩

召唤我,使我清醒
不能轻易脱掉自己的装束
面对现实,需要保护
继续用体面的衣裳包裹

我本不再需要什么
只想沉浸于这闪亮的一刻
放弃不合情理的失魂
慢慢地,慢慢与沿途的风景同行

人生没有最完美的形式
喝一杯清茶,吃一口淡饭
读一本好书,听一首老歌
摒弃自私而古老的平庸

夜行高速,空灵而狂野
仿若地球自身的黑色丝线
负重,被光索牵引
在伟大和平凡的边缘,展现
不平凡的执着

(2017年8月23日处暑夜,于上海回绍兴高速公路上)

Night travel on the expressways, flexible and wild.
I felt as if they were the earth's black silk threads.
Load bearing, pulled by the light rope.
Was shown on the edge of greatness and ordinariness,
Extraordinary persistence.

(On the night of August 23, 2017, the Limit of Heat, On the expressway from Shanghai to Shaoxing)

Pedestrian Street in Summer

Summer belongs to women and migrant workers, bareness and laziness;
It belongs to the boring frogs and the helpless cicadas;
It belongs to a cup of old wine and naked feet;
It belongs to the drinks in the freezer,
And the homework books on the small table in front of the store.

The street is not long, just like summer not baking the earth for long.
A few antique painting and calligraphy stores, framing the classics of the street.
The stone pillar gatehouses and old-fashioned doors record the city's age.
A song *The Jiangnan Region of Rivers and Lakes*, with the noise of sprinklers,
Reveal how the hustle and bustle of this ancient town is.
I go on, stopping from time to time, either reminiscing or searching.

夏天的步行街

夏天属于女人和民工，属于裸露和慵懒
属于无聊的蛙声和无奈的蝉鸣
属于一碗老酒和赤裸的双脚
属于冰柜里的饮料
还有店铺门口小板桌上的作业本

小街并不长，就像夏天不会对大地长久地炙烤
几家古董字画铺，装裱着这条街的古典
石柱门楼和老式排门，记录着这座城市的年轮
一曲"江南水乡"，夹着洒水车的噪音
诉说着这座城市的喧闹和古老
我走一走停一停，不知是在回味还是寻找

The eyeglass store in the street has a stylish facade like the face of Ultraman.
The coffee bar in the center of the street compete with the fried stinky tofu.
The old green stone bridge is the best view here.
This place is an extension of Lu Xun's hometown;
This place is adjacent to the clamouring South Jiefang Road;
Here you can smell the fragrance of ink and the sound of crying children.

Which can break through the summer heaven, a few bottles of beer,
Or the cloth curtain blocking the sun?
Take a look at your health first, goodbye;
The pedestrian street, no need to come back for a walk.
The gray top of the tower on the Ta Mountain, supporting a sky on fire.
I'm going to take off your modern jacket in the summer heat,
I want to wake up your sleeping soul in a light—hearted laugh.
You are an old street, you are a famous town.

眼镜店站立街中,时尚的门面像奥特曼脸谱
咖啡吧落于街心,誓与油炸臭豆腐争宠
青石老桥是这里的最佳风景
这里延伸着鲁迅故里的风情
这里与解放南路的喧嚣比邻
这里能闻到墨香,这里有小孩的哭声

谁能冲破夏天的酷热,几瓶啤酒
还是遮挡着太阳的布帘
先打量一下自己的身体,再见
步行街,不必再来走一个轮回
塔山上的灰色塔顶,支撑着一个火烧的天空
我要在夏天的热浪中,脱掉你现代的外套
我要在轻松的笑谈中,催醒你沉睡的灵魂
你是一条老街,你是一座名城

Moonlight on the Huansha River

You are the radiance that came from the Spring and
   Autumn period,
Hanging in the distant starry sky.
Silently dripping into the river,
Rippling tirelessly
For the night in the hometown of Xishi.
You are the wild gull that wakes up the river,
Posing to kiss every wave.
You are also like a Chinese trumpet creeper,
Climbing on the green riverbank.
The moonlight from the ancient time,
With the fragrance of the beauty of the Yue Kingdom,
Over and over again
Illuminating every inch of my skin.

You are like a flock of doves of peace,
Harmoniously perching in the canopy of trees and lawns.
In the evening when the autumn wind blow,
You guard peace and tranquility,

浣纱江的月光

你是从春秋时期走来的光辉
悬挂在遥远的星空
悄悄地滴入江中
为西施故里的夜晚
荡起不倦的涟漪
你是唤醒江面的野鸥
像要吻遍每一朵浪花
又像是凌霄花
攀援在翠绿的江堤
来自远古的月光啊
带着越国美女的芳香
一遍又一遍
将我的每一寸肌肤照亮

你像是一群和平鸽
和谐地栖息在树冠和草坪
在秋风升起的傍晚
守护着和平与安宁

Like a salute to the blue sky.

You are more like an tercel,

In the silence of the night,

Swooping down from the height of faith,

Letting me see the power of truth.

The moonlight on the Huansha River,

Carrying the hopes and ideals of the people in my hometown,

Again and again

Calling me back to my hometown from my sleepy dreams.

像礼花为蓝天绽放
你更像是一只雄鹰
在寂静的夜色里
从信仰的高度俯冲而下
让我看到真理的力量
浣纱江上的月光啊
带着家乡人民的希冀和理想
一次又一次
将我从沉睡的梦中唤回故乡

The Morning Sun of the Xixiao River

Dawn, break free from dreams.

The process of congestion slowly approaches.

An old and agile river,

Flowing quietly in the blood of the ancient city.

The black-topped boat sails gently,

Opening up the charming breasts of the ancient city.

Gradually revealing a faint pink hue,

Shyly preparing for a day of nurturing.

The water is sparkling, shooting the yellowing street scene.

The Xixiao River, a meek child's pet name,

Was born at the same time as the Yue Kingdom.

At sunset, it is charming, and at sunrise, it is fascinating.

Smoke rises up with dreams,

Awakening the lazy and lonely window pane.

晨 曦
——写在绍兴西小河

晨曦,从梦境中挣脱出来
充血的过程缓慢来临
一条苍老灵动的小河
在古城的血脉里静静流淌

乌篷船轻轻划过
掀开了古都娇媚的丰乳
渐渐裸露出淡淡的绯红
羞涩地准备一天的哺育

水波粼粼,拍摄泛黄街景
西小河,一个温顺的乳名
与古代越国同时出生
日落妩媚,日出荧魂

炊烟带着梦想袅袅升起
唤醒了慵懒寂寞的窗棂

The sound of tinkling water
Still plays a lingering melody.

The willow lures the brightness of the creek,
Softly lapping the backs of pedestrians.
The green stone slabs precipitate the vicissitudes of history,
Carefully recording the hurried footprints.

The stone lions on the bridge show their might,
Guarding the tranquility of the creek.
The curved holes of the bridge reveal a sweet smile,
Decorating the classical and tender feelings of the river.

The sunlight penetrates the mist,
Beginning to shine brightly.
The flame in the heart of the river
Burns reverently downward.
The little river is lit up, the little river smiles.

叮咚的流水声
依旧弹奏着缠绵的旋律

柳条引诱着小河的光明
柔软地拍打着行人的背影
青石板沉淀着历史的沧桑
细心记录下匆匆的脚印

桥上的石狮装显着威武
守护着小河的安宁
弯弯的桥洞露出甜甜的笑容
装点着小河的古典与柔情

阳光穿透了薄雾
开始闪着耀眼的光芒
小河泛起了心中的火焰
虔诚地向下燃烧
小河亮了,小河笑了

Twilight in Lu Xun's Hometown

Walking past the corner of the curved ruler-like counter,

The lamp of Xianheng Restaurant

Has already lit up the dusk.

The Xiucai Kong pretended to be civilized.

My calm footsteps measured it,

Splitting time into two centuries.

Do not detour from the subject,

Only talk about the word "early" engraved in the Sanwei Study,

Rather than about the mulberries in the Baicao Garden,

I increasingly can't understand

The story of the Zhou's Compound.

Xianglin's Wife cannot live here,

With the "Sacrifice" of "Medicine", she should move slowly.

黄　昏
——写在绍兴鲁迅故里

　　　　走过曲尺柜台的转角
　　　　"咸亨酒店"的灯
　　　　已经点亮了黄昏
　　　　孔秀才酸溜溜装着斯文
　　　　我从容的脚步丈量着
　　　　将时间分割成两个世纪

　　　　不要绕开主题
　　　　只聊刻在三味书屋的"早"字
　　　　不谈百草园里的桑葚
　　　　越来越读不懂
　　　　周家台门的故事
　　　　祥林嫂不在这里安生
　　　　带着药的祝福应该缓行

It's not an accidental encounter

The blacked-topped boat is paddled with the tinkling sound of water,

Carrying Lu Xun back to his hometown to visit his relatives.

Seeing Lu Xun in western clothes,

Brother Runtu was like a Tofu Xishi,

Expressionless and mute.

The stone road is bumpy,

And is lined with bamboo silk gates with pink walls and tiles of blackish tint.

The traces of the old days are still intact,

No gentlemen in a long coat walk by,

Only those in blue pants and flowered skirts

Move in their own shadows,

Leading the Earth Temple to the coldness.

Under the Renli archway,

The stinky tofu is fried to a crisp and sizzling smell in the street.

I sit at an eight immortals' table at the Shou Family Compound,

并不是偶然的邂逅
乌篷船划出叮咚的水声
载着先生回故乡探亲
闰土阿弟见了穿西服的先生
犹如豆腐西施一般
木讷得毫无表情

石板路凹凸有致
两边的竹丝台门粉墙黛瓦
依然保持着旧时的痕迹
没有穿长衫的先生走过
只有蓝裤子花裙子
挽着自己的影子款款而行
领着"土谷祠"走向冷清

臭豆腐在"仁里"牌坊下
炸得吱吱啦啦满街飘香
我坐在"寿家台门"的八仙桌旁

An expired business card

Is stuck in the middle of *Diary of a Madman*.

With the change in the corner of the bag,

I buy half a pot of old wine.

Inspired by the spirit of Ah Q,

I drink up the fatigue of the day,

Quietly watching the row of doors according to the street being closed.

一张过期的名片
夹在了《狂人日记》中间
用袋角的零钱
换来半壶老酒
在阿Q精神鼓舞下
饮尽了一天疲劳
静观对面排门落下

Echoes of South Second Beltway of Shaoxing

The South Second Beltway in the early morning

Is always woken up by the wail.

Knocking and beating, near and far

To bid farewell to the deceased,

Another grand occasion is held in his honor.

The paper cones ring toward the sky,

Which is a salute to the road to heaven.

Smoothly making the faraway place less far

For the soul on the way to the netherworld.

There is no need to come to the South Second Ring Road in advance for the race.

Although the medicine of eternal life has not yet been found,

Life can grow old slowly.

The lotus flowers on the roadside enter the muddy pond,

Turning green again and again,

回　声
——写在绍兴二环南路

清晨的二环南路
总是被哀号吵醒
敲敲打打，忽远忽近
为告别人间的亡者
再作一次隆重的挽留报道
纸筒朝天鸣响
是去往天堂之路的礼炮
为赶往黄泉路上的魂灵
顺利送往远方之远的远方

不必提前来二环南路赛跑
长生之药虽未找到
人生可以慢慢变老
路边荷花入泥塘
绿了又绿

Yellow and yellow again,
The cycle of life is exactly the same.

Don't get excited when you pick up a glass of wine,
It's only the alcohol that ignites the blood,
Impulsively beating your chest,
Boasting about friendship that is plausibly true and false,
Or meaningless commitment.

A fortune-telling master lies,
Only he himself knows about them the best.
How hard it is if you cannot fall asleep at midnight.
Astrological horoscope is just a floating cloud,
What you have will be lost eventually,
What you long for will come again.

Living in a bustling city,
Don't think too much about the world.
The originality of the fields
Is a temporary luxury,
And is not there every weekend.
The hundred beauties in the heart
Secretly collide with imagination for countless times.

黄了又黄

生命的轮回一模一样

不要端起酒杯就血气方刚

无非是酒精点燃了血液

冲动地拍着胸膛

高论真假参半的友谊

或者毫无意义的担当

算命大师谎言一套

只有自己最懂得

午夜难以入睡何等难熬

星座运程都是浮云

拥有的终将失去

渴望的还会来到

生活在繁华的都市里

俗念不要过于纵横

田野里的原生态

是一种暂时的奢华

不是每个周末都能兑现

内心的百媚

无数次与想象偷偷碰撞

In the evening on the South Second Beltway,

Hot dance music starts to play.

Old men and women dance in the twilight of joy,

Indicating that our people like to have a good time,

Reminding the master of life that

Life is so simple.

It's either the joy of dusk

Or the wail of the morning.

傍晚的二环南路
热烈的舞曲开始播放
大叔大妈跳着喜悦的黄昏
诉说着咱老百姓喜欢热闹
提醒着生命的主人
生活就是如此简单
要么是黄昏的喜悦
要么是清晨的哀号

Street Lamp at the NO.1 Water Street in Shaoxing

I move into 1 Water Street at the invitation of the night,
The cold shadows of the trees count my footsteps.
Listening to the cicadas calling from afar,
The lake can no longer illuminate the reflection of people.

Tonight, I can only go forward with my fantasy.
After the busy and tiring daytime,
People have closed their eyes.
At this moment, I am happy to accompany the quietness,
My heart silently holds on to a belief:
May you find a ray of light in my thoughts.

When I wake up, I may not see your smile,
When I leave, you will look back and survey.
You can't understand the arrangement of this era,
Leaving me alone with you in solitude.
I always remember the glow of your goodbyes,
At the last light,
We each chose our own directions,
I was destined to be alone in the shadows of the night.

路 灯
——写在绍兴水街一号

夜色的邀请,走进水街一号
冷清的树影,数着我的脚步
倾听知了呼唤着远方
湖水已经照不出人的倒影

今晚,只能带着幻想前行
在白昼的忙碌劳累过后
人们早已闭上了眼睛
此刻,我快乐地陪伴着宁静
心中默默坚守着一个信念
愿你在我的思绪里找到一线光明

当我醒来,或许看不到你的微笑
当我离开,你会回过头来打量
你无法理解这个时代的安排
让我和你独自孤独地生活
我总是记起你道别时的神采飞扬
在上一个灯下
我们选择了各自的方向
注定了,我在夜影下的孤单

The Silk Shop at Noon

At summer noon, it was forty-one degrees Celsius,
The high temperature passionately burned the soles of shoes red.
Inside the counter, colorful silks filled the room,
The dangling colors lost their confident floating.
There is no wind, the air is motionless,
Baking the lightness of this fabric of the South of Yangtze River.

You do not have a famous family's pedigree,
but have a noble heart.
Each silk thread
holds a moth that likes to flutter the fire.
Each piece of color
Wraps an enchanting and restless heart,
Searching for winds in the season of jumping.

正午时的丝绸屋

夏日正午,摄氏四十一度
高温热情地将鞋底烫红
柜台内,多彩的丝绸满屋
悬垂着的色彩失去了自信的飘逸
没有风,空气纹丝不动
烘烤着这种江南面料的轻薄

没有名门的血统
却有高贵的心性
每一根丝线
都牵着一只喜欢扑火的飞蛾
每一块色彩
都裹着一颗妖娆不安分的心
在跳跃的季节里采风

The silk shop at midday

Surrounded and overwhelmed by the heat outside the counter.

There were no customers, it was a little lonely.

O colorful silk! Your gracefulness

Came from the cocoons produced in darkness.

Your silky delicacy,

Your softness and peaceful beauty

Are inclusive to the pain of the air moving and staying static,

And enriching the lonely and quiet shop.

正午时的丝绸屋

被柜台外的热浪包围淹没

无人问津，略显孤独

多彩的丝绸啊！你的婀娜

源自黑暗的作茧自缚

你丝丝相扣的细腻

你柔柔祥和的绚美

包容着，空气动静间的疼痛

丰富着，寂寞冷清的小屋

Meditation on the Celebrity Square

On the stone sculptures in the Celebrity Square,
They are all still alive.
The Yu the Great, Goujian, Ma Zhen, Wang Xizhi,
Lu You, Xu Wei, Qiu Jin, Lu Xun,
Cai Yuanpei, Zhu Kezhen, Zhou Enlai
These sages, who stood on the high ground of history,
Came all the way from the source of the ancient Yue Kingdom
To modern civilization,
Made sensational accomplishment in a big way,
Awakening the people and benefiting humanity.
I look up at them and bow my head in thought.

They held the steering wheel that drive the wheel of history,
Digging canals, cutting cliffs and living on rivers with hills as pillows,

沉 思
——写在绍兴名人广场

名人广场的石雕上
他们都还活着
大禹、勾践、马臻、王羲之
陆游、徐渭、秋瑾、鲁迅
蔡元培、竺可桢、周恩来
这些站在历史的高处
从古越源头而来
连接着现代文明的圣贤
拨动山水,翻覆云雨
惊醒世人,造福人类
我抬头仰视,低头沉思

他们手握推动历史车轮的方向盘
开渠凿壁,枕山依水

Reflecting the essence of the world,
Leading the trend of human civilization.
Countless footsteps and admiring eyes,
Move from Xuantingkou to the corner of Qingteng Book House,
From the Jiezhu Temple to the renaissance of Zhejiang University after its resettlement in Guizhou Province during Anti-Japanese War,
Immersed in the chords of the Yu the Great fighting floods,
Standing on the Fu Hill where Goujian slept on sticks and tasted gall.

I entered the square with reverence
To see their greatness and uprightness.
I suddenly felt that I was being watched by them,
Their eyes directing at my humility,
Hitting me by my weaknesses.
I slowed down my steps,
I didn't know if it was shyness or paleness,
I had to bury my figure.

映照天地日月之精华
引领人类文明之潮流
无数前行的脚步与瞻仰的目光
从轩亭口走到青藤书屋的拐角处
从戒珠寺跨越浙江大学西迁复兴
浸润在大禹治水的和弦里
站立在卧薪尝胆的府山上

我用崇敬的心情走进广场
观览他们的伟岸和挺拔
我忽然觉得反被他们观览
目光直射向我的卑微
击中我的软肋
我放慢自己的脚步
不知是羞涩,还是苍白
不得不将自己的身影掩埋

In front of the statue of the sages,

I stared and collected my feelings.

"Moving east to Japan following 'The Internationale' on
   the Songhua River."

"A Woman with a phoenix hairpin" in the Shen's Garden,

"Head bowed, like a willing ox I serve the children."

Dike was built by the governor to create Jing Lake.

The wisdom of great men carried on by their successors

Fell like meteorite stars near to me,

Disturbing my description,

Smashing the shallow lines of poetry.

I prayed with all my heart

That in this square where the sages live,

There will be only reverence, no harassment.

Leave behind the bewitching colors of the landscape,

Store it in the world, bear it in mind,

As an inexhaustible source of food for thought.

在圣人雕像的面前
我凝望着拾起自己的情怀
"大江歌罢调头东"
沈氏园里钗头凤
"俯首甘为孺子牛"
太守筑堤创镜湖
伟人的智慧,后人的传承
陨石星子般从身边落下
惊扰了我的描述
砸断了浅浅的诗行

我虔诚地祈祷
祈祷这座圣人居住的广场
只有敬仰,没有骚扰
抛却山光水色的妖艳
存储于世,扎根于心
积蓄取之不尽的食粮

Morning in An Alley

A burst of hawking went on.
Amidst the noise, I looked for
The old house with stone stools at the door.
Fried dough sticks and soybean milk gave me a sense of
 of warmth,
Bringing up my childhood memories.
She and I were childhood lovers and our get—together was
 like a dream.

A few galleries and stalls of antiques
Decorate the modernity of the alley,
And embellish the antiquity of the alley.
It is suitable for seclusion and small talk.
Retaining old visitors who come back at any time,
Waiting for the overture dedicated to the years.

Suit does not match with a woolen felt hat,
Pink walls is decorated with oil paper umbrellas.
The sunrise hits the green stone slab,

小巷的早晨

一阵阵叫卖,一声声吆喝
嘈杂之中,寻找
门口摆着石凳的老屋
油条豆浆,浮起一幕温情
浮出,我的童年
两小无猜,佳期如梦

几家画廊,几摊古玩
装饰着小巷的现代
点缀着小巷的古朴
适合隐居,适合闲聊
时刻挽留归来的老客
等待献给岁月的序曲

西装,配不上乌毡帽
粉墙,装点着油纸伞
朝阳打在青石板上

Faintly glowing,

Reflecting the bustling alleys,

Reflecting the figures of young children leaving home.

Who said that love is one person's waiting?

The alley is harmonious,

The alley is not lonely.

Alley people are happy for a long time,

None of them cries for their breakup.

The alley is older than modern people.

Step gently through a century,

This is a long—awaited reunion.

Like the colors of spring, it blooms in the streets.

The pedestrians flowing through the corners of my eyes are déjà vu.

Strange tugs at the sleeves of time,

The eyes and the heart are slowly drenched.

The women who passed by were modern,

Leaving behind a view of their elegant backs in a hurry.

A breeze stirred up the song of the alley.

I was reminiscing, I wanted to embrace.

泛起隐隐光辉
映照着熙熙攘攘的小巷
映红了少小离家的身影

谁说,爱是一个人的等候
小巷和气融融
小巷并不寂寞
小巷人幸福长久
小巷没有人哭着分手
小巷比现代人更加悠久

脚步轻轻,踏过了一个世纪
这是一次久别的重逢
像春天的色彩,绽放街头
流过眼角的行人,似曾相识
陌生,拽住了时光的衣袖
让眼睛与心灵慢慢湿透

身旁飘过的女郎,摩登
匆匆地,留下飘逸的背影
一阵清风,撩起小巷的欢歌
我在回味,我想拥抱

Reminiscing the freshness of the sunlight,
Embracing the beautiful morning in the alley.
Someone laughed and asked, "Where do you come from?"
I looked at the alley and felt like I'd never left.

The white cane clicked with the laughter of questioning.
Hometown is in the South of Yangtze River, there is no need to cross the hills.
The Lotus Flower Melody in different Localities is not an ancient symbol.
Walking through the alley, my feet were covered with dew.
I don't know if I'm moving faster or slower.
Looking down, it's a deep longing,
Looking back, it's a warm life.

回味穿透阳光的清新
拥抱小巷和美的早晨
有人笑问,你从何处来
我望着小巷,感觉从未离开过

白手杖,点击着问询的笑声
故乡是江南,不必越过山丘
莲花落不是古老的象征
走尽小巷,脚面沾满了露水
不知是快了还是慢了一拍
低头,是深深的思念
回首,是温暖的人生

The Poetic Soul of the Grand Canal

In the name of poetry, the oar
Wakes up the sleeping Grand Canal.
Clear, dynamic,
Wide and magnificent,
Like a giant dragon,
Embellishing the landscape of the ancient Yue Kingdom,
Drunk in the wind and moon of Kuaiji.

In front of my eyes, the blue water is flooded with waves,
By the ears, poetry stirs.
The boat moves past the mountains full of greenery.
Voices nostalgia, bursts of nostalgia,
The 800 li of Jing Lake in crowded months and years.
After seeing Li Bai sail far,
It had Meng Haoran's boat passing by.

What kind of immortal mountain and divine water
Made the Chinese Bard and the great scholars drunkenly sing?

大运河的诗魂

船橹以诗的名义
摇醒了沉睡的大运河
清澈,灵动
宽阔,恢宏
似一条巨龙
点缀古越山水
醉卧会稽风月

眼前,碧水泛波
耳畔,诗情骚动
船行山移,满目苍翠
一声声乡音,一阵阵乡愁
镜湖八百里,峥嵘岁月稠
才送李太白衣襟远航
又与孟浩然扁舟擦过

何等的仙山神水
引来诗圣大儒醉酒放歌

Tang poems praise its great beauty,
Song ci-poems record its classics.
The Shen's Garden, Wozhou Lake,
The Tianmu Mountain, the Ruoye River.
I'm visiting Lanting today,
The Xishipu in the distance also seems to be covered with a hazy veil,
But I will return through the Shanxi River.

The Grand Canal flows through the ancient Yue Wonderland,
It also flows through the heart me, a passerby.
A simple pen comes from the source of history
To enlighten the hometown, righteous and upright.
I brush away the white clouds in the sky with my hand;
I rise with the sound of sculling and stand on the prow of the boat.
The autumn breeze combs the custom-made hair.
I straighten my lapel and shake my sleeves,
Raising the flame, with the soul of poetry
To praise history and ignite the light.

唐诗赞誉着大美

宋词记载着经典

沈氏园,沃洲湖

天姥山,若耶水

今日赠予兰亭去

西施浦上更飘纱

却绕剡溪回

大运河,流过古越仙境

也流过我——过客的心头

一支素笔从历史源头伸来

点化故乡,义正气昂

手拂天上白云飘过

随橹声而起,站立船头

秋风梳理着定制的发型

我整一整衣襟,抖一抖衣袖

举起火焰,用诗歌的灵魂

点赞历史,点燃光芒

Record

The Evening of Lanting

The evening of Lanting is beautiful.

The Lanting Preface was beautifully written.

Two thousand years have elapsed,

The Lanting Pavilion and Tablet

Are beautiful against the blooming lotus flowers.

White geese play in the water,

Light and airy,

Singing to the sky.

Rippling soft waves,

Dances in the water are beautiful.

The literati meet

At a winding stream party.

They drank and composed poems,

Creating a legend of poems in Chinese.

The Lanting Preface is beautiful.

记　载
——兰亭的傍晚

兰亭的傍晚很美

书法很美

岁月沧桑记载了两个千年

亭子和碑

衬托着绽放的荷花很美

白鹅,在水中嬉戏

轻盈飘逸

仰天放歌

荡漾起片片柔波

舞蹈在水中很美

文人墨客相聚

曲水流觞

诗酒歌赋

醉美了方块字的千古传奇

那篇"集序"很美

The small bamboo leaves cover the sunset,
The quaint Lanting
Deified the charm of Chinese character art.
The aura of the dragon dancing calligraphy
Dances and hovers in the endless years.

小小的竹叶掩映着夕阳
古朴的兰亭
神化了汉字艺术的魅力
龙跳法的灵气
在无尽的岁月中飞舞盘旋

Goose Pond

Cloaked in snowflakes, geese frolic,

Chanting with lovers in the pond,

Chanting for their own nobility, singing for the elegance of nature.

Covered by the graceful bamboo,

Accompanied by the peaceful and relaxing meadow.

Countless wanderers approach you,

You smile up at the sky, only intoxicated by yourself.

You have been through the heat and cold of the world, laughing at the changes,

You spread your wings awesomely, rippling the clear waves.

The Lanting Preface has been eulogized for thousands of years.

You bend your neck toward the sky, your white plumes float on the water.

Your lasting charm will stand rock—firm and high.

O Goose Pond! I can't remember

In which century your legend began.

鹅　池

披着一身雪花,嬉戏
在池塘里,与情侣吟唱
吟自己的高洁,唱自然的风雅
仪态万方的翠竹掩映
宁静悠然的草地作伴
数不清的游人,走近了你
你仰天一笑,只顾自己陶醉

历经炎凉世态,笑看风云变幻
风骨展翅,清波涟漪
《兰亭集序》风流千古
曲项昂扬向天,白羽优雅浮水
流芳后世的神韵,合璧矗立

鹅池啊！我记不清
你的传说,始于哪个世纪

Wang Xizhi liked you, which naturally proves your incomparable beauty.
A boat sails on swiftly,
Huangting Classics are sought by Daoists.
White geese like singing,
The Sage of Calligraphy has remained famous since ancient times.

Your aura
Has nourished generations of great masters and the Sage of Calligraphy,
Nurtured the spirit of the dragon jumping method,
Embellished the charm of the winding stream party.
You have retained your youthful aura for over a millennium
And deified the charm of Chinese character art.

You are the monument of Chinese calligraphy.
Standing on the pyramid of Oriental civilization,
I don't need to genuflect and kiss your feet,
Nor do I need to miss you day and night and praise you loudly.
I only need to wait in silence with my pure heart,
For your strength, your spontaneity and your beauty.

右军喜欢,自然艳美无比
一叶扁舟轻帆卷
黄庭真经道家求
换白鹅,喜善鸣
惜福书圣,扬名今昔

你的灵气
滋养了一代代宗师书圣
点化了龙跳法的传神
点缀了曲水流觞的魅力
沧桑千年,依然青春灵动
神化了方块字的艺术真谛

你是一撇一捺搭载的丰碑
站立在东方文明的金字塔上
我不必跪下吻你的双脚
也无需日夜想念,高声赞赏
只需捧出一颗赤心,默默守候
你的苍劲,你的奔放,你的秀美

Seeing the Puyang River Again

The Puyang River, I see you again.
An ancient and mysterious, familiar yet strange hometown.
Your fortitude and tenderness
Have nurtured the life and history of Jiyang City,
And Fostered the generosity and affection of Jiyang people.

The green river bank smiles,
With its broad shoulders open wide,
Waiting for her children to come home from a long journey like a mother.
The flying doves gently call the setting sun,
Looking forward to tomorrow's new sunshine.

The Puyang River, I see you again.
New—style neighborhoods stand on both sides,
Like a new bride emitting the fragrance of flowers,
Showing the value and power of life.
Myths and unofficial histories have become passing clouds,
Only your love and beauty are perpetually.

又见浦阳江

浦阳江,我又见到了你
古老又神秘,熟悉又陌生的故乡
你的刚毅和柔情
孕育了暨阳城的生命和历史
培育了暨阳人的宽宏和情义

翠绿的江堤微笑着
敞开着宽阔的肩膀
慈母般地等待远行的子女回家
飞翔的鸽子轻轻呼唤着落日
期盼着明日新的阳光

浦阳江,我又见到了你
新式街区屹立两岸
像新嫁娘散发着花香
展示着生命的价值和力量
神话和野史都成了烟云
只有你的爱和美才是永恒

We Still Have an Appointment

More and more like a smartphone,

Mute, everything is silent,

Only air and moisture caress,

Slowly fade away until it's a stone thrown from the sky,

And end up in old age.

Turn on, like a rain of enthusiasm,

Crackling, jumping the the passing and present

Origins.

It's a group of people who come ashore with the help of
   the flowing water,

Say goodbye to the increasingly dull routine life,

Suddenly gather together,

Reunited with laughter in the world of mortals.

I want to ask:

Shall we agree on an afterlife?

When we were young students,

我们还有约定

越来越像一部智能手机
静音,一切都是沉寂的
只有空气和水分轻抚
缓慢地淡忘,直到咫尺天涯
老态龙钟
开机,似一场雨的热烈
噼噼啪啪,跳跃着过往的当下的
缘起

是一群扶着流水上岸的人
辞别愈加寥落的日常
突然聚拢在一起
滚滚红尘中欢笑着重逢

我想问
我们要约定来世吗
恰同学少年

A lifetime of friendship was still a little too short, a little too thin,
Too many pieces of warmth were taken away,
Less was brought by the pieces of delicateness.

I want to ask:
Shall we agree on an afterlife?
We were born and raised in the same place, nourished by the same rain,
The mountains are small in our eyes, the sun and moon are light in our heart.
We are all friends,
Cups of yellow wine are still warm, the battlefield of childhood is in full swing.
Turn around to find the world far and wide,
We still have an appointment.

友爱一生还是短了一些,单薄了一些
温馨的点点滴滴带走的多了一些
精致的丝丝缕缕带来的更少了一些

我想问
我们要约定来世吗
我们在一地生养,一雨滋润
眼底江山小,胸中淡日月
与子同袍
一杯黄酒尚温,童年的战场正酣
转身的江湖迢迢
我们还有约定

We Were Separated Only by the Distance between Desks

To my dear classmates

  We

Were separately only by the distance between desks.

Not too far, not too close,

Unbiased and impartial.

I yearn;

You pursued.

  We

Were separately only by the distance between desks.

With the whisper of flowing water,

With the rise and fall of the mountains.

I listened;

You talked.

  We

Were separately only by the distance between desks.

Vines of five thousand years,

我们，只有课桌间的距离
——以此献给亲爱的同学们

我们
只有课桌间的距离
不远不近
不偏不倚
憧憬是我
追寻是你

我们
只有课桌间的距离
以流水的细语
以山峦的起伏
聆听是我
倾诉是你

我们
只有课桌间的距离
五千年的藤蔓

Crawled along the books.
I chewed;
You absorbed.

We
Were separately only by the distance between desks.
Just like the ancient towpaths along banks or in river,
The water and the sky extended as far as our eyes could see.
I was expansive;
You were classical.

We
Were separately only by the distance between desks.
I used the texture of mountains and rivers,
To draw your long hair and beautiful clothes.
I were happy;
You were pleased.

We
Were separately only by the distance between desks.
On the palette of the years,
There was the sound of gurgling water.

沿着书本而来
咀嚼的是我
吸收的是你

我们
只有课桌间的距离
就像临水依岸或破水而筑的古纤道
水天极目之处
辽阔是我
古典是你

我们
只有课桌间的距离
我用山河的纹理
绘制你的长发锦衣
乐的是我
喜的是你

我们
只有课桌间的距离
岁月的调色板上
有了潺潺的流水声

The blue was me;

The red was you.

We

Were separately only by the distance between desks.

We met before sunrise,

We parted at sunset.

I moved on;

You were graceful.

We

Were separately only by the distance between desks.

In the alley too narrow an umbrella to be carried,

I put away my umbrella.

I was happy;

You were elegant.

We

Were separately only by the distance between desks.

Like black letters not written on a sheet of white paper,

Seeing the shyness but not the sorrowful sobbing.

I was infatuated;

You were pure.

蓝颜是我

红颜是你

我们

只有课桌间的距离

在日出前相遇

在落日时话别

赶路的是我

婀娜的是你

我们

只有课桌间的距离

在支不开伞的弄堂里

我收起油伞

怡情是我

优雅是你

我们

只有课桌间的距离

像白纸上没有写上黑字

看见羞晕却看不见忧伤的抽泣

痴情是我

清纯是你

We

Were separately only by the distance between desks.

Your rose was left in my dream;

My flower season materialized with your charming.

I was elegant;

You were fragrant.

We

Were separately only by the distance between desks.

I liked the breeze, the moon and the sunshine;

You liked the fragrance of flowers, birdsong and red haze.

I was touched;

You were grateful.

We

Were separately only by the distance between desks.

You were a lotus flower in the lake;

I was a young lotus root out of the mud.

Even though,

Our white paper has been filled with weed−like black letters,

With question marks like bows,

我们

只有课桌间的距离

你的玫瑰遗落在我的梦里

我的花季成了你的旖旎

飘逸是我

芳香是你

我们

只有课桌间的距离

我喜欢清风、明月、阳光

你喜欢花香、鸟鸣、红霞

感动是我

感恩是你

我们

只有课桌间的距离

你是湖中莲花

我是嫩藕出泥

即使

我们的白纸已经住满杂草般的黑字

问号般躬下了腰身

With the comma—like pain of the past,

The moonlight of the city and the half—tree birdsong,

Still remain in the passing time.

Looking at the stream in the mountains, listening to the tide of the sea,

You interpret perfection with your theme,

I use my exclamation point to write a legend.

逗号般疼痛的过往
那一城月色，半树鸟鸣
还留在流逝的时光里
看山间的溪水，听大海的潮声
你用你的主题诠释完美
我用我的叹号谱写传奇

A Salute to Teachers

To teachers at Teachers' Day

Today is a special day,
It's your red-letter day, my dear teachers.
Let us offer you a bunch of flowers,
To express our respect to you.
Let us present you a short poem,
To express the heartfelt gratitude of your students.

Your generous heart,
Embraces all that we are.
Your deep wisdom,
Enlightens our minds.
Your profound knowledge,
Baptizes our souls.

You lead us,
To climb one ladder after another.
You use your dais,

向老师敬礼
——在教师节献给老师

今天,是个特别的日子
是你的节日——我亲爱的老师
让我们献上一束鲜花
表达心中对你的敬意
用一首小诗
道出同学们由衷的感激

你宽广的胸怀
将我们的一切包容
你深沉的智慧
将我们的思想启迪
你渊博的知识
将我们的心灵洗礼

你引领着我们
带上一个又一个攀登的阶梯
你用讲台

To solve one problem after another.
You taught us by example,
Encouraging us not to bow our heads in the face of difficulties.
For months and for years,
You cultivated and nurtured us,
So that we could grow up to be the elite of society.
All year round,
You worked hard and give selflessly,
Without wanting to take anything from us.

Ah! Beloved teachers:
In so many holidays,
Have you left your solid footprints around your students,
And imprinted your beautiful images on our hearts.
This has become our permanent memory.
We cannot forget you,
And we will never forget you.

You helped us to achieve excellent results,
You gave us the courage to live.
You taught us the truth of being a human being,

解答了人生中一个又一个难题
你言传身教
鼓励我们在困难面前不要把头低
寒来暑往,星转斗移
你默默耕耘精心培育
让同学们成长为社会精英
春夏秋冬,一年四季
你辛劳付出无私奉献
不计回报从不索取

啊！敬爱的老师
多少节假的日子
你把坚实的足迹留在同学们身边
你把美好的形象印在我们的心里
镌刻成永久的记忆
我们不能忘记你
我们也不会忘记

你帮助我们获取了优异的成绩
你给我们增添了生活的勇气
你教我们懂得了做人的道理

You gave us the motivation to move forward again and again.
You, beloved teachers,
Are the idols in our hearts,
And our eternal friends.
On this special day,
We salute you!

使我们一次次有了前进的动力
你,敬爱的老师
我们心中的偶像
我们永远的朋友
在今天这个特别的日子里
让我们行一个端端正正的礼

Thou

To my teacher, Madam Xia

With a pair of ordinary small hands,

You built a bridge of knowledge.

At one end of the bridge is the giant of the East,

At the other end is the center of Europe.

UBI[①] welcomed me

To the European continent in search of our dreams.

From cold winter

To hot summer,

You held up the sky of the Kingdom of Knowledge,

Guiding the way to the Kingdom of Knowledge.

You led people with a vision

In traveling far and wide

To climb higher peaks.

You are tall, beautiful and confident.

---

① It is an internationally renowned school of business education.

你
——献给夏老师

你,一双平凡的小手
架起了一座知识的桥梁
桥的一端是东方巨人
另一端是欧洲中心
由此 UBI[①] 的大门迎接着
莘莘学子到欧洲大陆寻梦
从冬的严寒
到夏的酷暑
撑起了知识王国的天空
指点着知识王国的迷津

你,引领着有识之士
远涉重洋
攀登更高的山峰
挺拔、秀美、自信

---

① UBI 是一所国际知名商业教育学院。

Your white shirt under your beautiful hair
Is like the white cloud in the blue sky.
You are ethereal and elegant,
Dreamy and charming.
Your voice,
Like a bottle of time—honored Moutai spirit,
Is soft, sweet and Intoxicated.
You stand above life,
You are the goddess in our hearts,
You are a beautiful and dazzling star.

Today, we sing for you,
Today, we wish you well.

秀发下的白色衬衣
似蓝天上的白云
飘逸而高雅
梦幻而迷人
发出的声音
似茅台年份酒一般
绵柔、甜润、醉人
你站在了生命之上
是我们心中的女神
是美丽耀眼的星

今天,我们为你歌唱
今天,我们为你祝福

Ode to Comrades in Arms

Comrade in arm

Is a special name.

It's both abstract and broad,

The abstractness is very broad,

The broadness is very abstract.

The abstractness contains blood relatives,

The broadness incorporates life.

It's louder,

And more charmful

Than any other names.

Comrade in arm

Represents the experience of having met before.

We fought for food in the military station,

We competed on the sporting court.

We were scolded during training,

We were criticized at squad meetings.

The military song in the formation:

It was loud and clear and neat.

战友颂

战友
是个特殊的名字
既抽象又广义
抽象的很广义
广义的很抽象
抽象的包含着血亲
广义的融入了生命
它比任何一个名字
更加响亮
更具魅力

战友
是曾经相遇过的经历
兵站里抢过饭
球场上呕过气
训练时挨过骂
班务会上受过批
队列中的军歌
既嘹亮又整齐

Attention, at ease, one, two, one:

Were our common marching orders.

Even if one day:

You are a high-ranking government official,

Or an ordinary person in society,

Those laughter and tears:

Are the images we share,

Will never be forgotten;

Will be etched in our hearts.

Comrade in arm

Is a unique feeling.

It's a partner in life and death,

It's a fraternal love,

It's someone you care about following demobilization,

It's someone you remember after demobilization.

No matter how long we have parted,

We always have a lot to say,

About the old days,

Either good,

Or bad events.

Each and every story,

立正、稍息、一二一
是我们共同的口令
就算有一天
你身居庙堂之高
或处江湖之远
那些笑和泪
都是我们共同的画面
终身难忘
铭刻心里

战友
是一种别样的情怀
是生死与共的伙伴
是情同手足的兄弟
是退伍后的牵挂
是转业后的回忆
无论离别多久
总有说不完的话
叙不完的旧
道不完的喜悦
诉不完的忧愁
点点滴滴

Represents our love and remembrance of the military camp,
With endless gratitude,
With true love forever.

Comrade in arm
Is a family member who shares the same meal together,
With no impurities from fame and fortune,
With no materialistic currents,
Only with the wide bed we shared together,
Only with the trenches we climbed together,
Only with the folding stools we sat on together,
Only with the sentry posts where we worked together,
Only with our shared flight trails,
Only with the journey we made together,
With purity and trueness,
Like a jade[①] pot of ice.

Comrade in arm
Is strong, aged wine.
The longer it's stored,

---

① In chinese culture, a jade stands for moon.

是对军营的眷恋和回味

感恩无限

真情永远

战友

是同吃一锅饭的亲人

没有名利的杂质

没有物欲的浊流

只有一起睡过的通铺

只有一起爬过的战壕

只有一起坐过的马扎

只有一起站过的哨位

只有一起飞过的航迹

只有一起走过的历程

至纯至真

玉壶① 冰清

战友

是一坛浓厚的陈酒

存放得越长

---

① 玉壶指月亮。

The longer the thoughts will last.

The strong meaning,

The refreshing aroma,

They make our hearts beat violently,

And move on,

When we enjoy a reunion.

They make us miss each other,

From the bottom of our hearts,

After we were apart.

Comrade in arm

Is an invaluable treasure.

When you are in adversity,

It's a blazing fire,

Which ignites your passion,

And lights up your journey.

When you are good times,

It's a spring of ice−cold water,

Which removes your impetuosity,

To restore your calmness.

In for a storm

It's the arm to support each other,

So we stand up together,

思念就会越久
那浓浓的意味
爽口的芳香
令我们相聚时
心潮澎湃
奔涌不息
使我们离别后
牵肠挂肚
晶莹剔透

战友
是一笔无尽的财富
逆境中
是一把烈火
点燃你的激情
照亮你的征程
顺境时
是一汪冰泉
除却你的狂躁
挽回你的冷静
风雨里
是相互搀扶的臂膀
一起挺直脊梁

And step more firmly.

Under the sun,

It's the white cloud in the blue sky,

It's the romantic rainbow after the rain.

It with lofty ideals,

With transparency of heart.

Comrade in arm

Is a symbol of an era,

Although the photos of us when we joined the army

Have yellowed,

Even after taking off the military uniform,

We still have dignity and honor,

And are full of pride.

Heeding the call of the motherland,

We are found

Wherever there is danger.

The needs of the people

Is the call for emergency assembly.

No matter when

And no matter where

We will go forward

Without complaint or regret

步伐更加坚定

阳光下

是蓝天上飘扬的白云

是雨后浪漫的彩虹

志存高远

心生透明

战友

是一个时代的象征

虽然入伍时的照片

已经泛黄

即便脱下了军装

依然正义凛然

豪气一身

听从祖国的召唤

哪里有险情

哪里就有我们的背影

人民的需要

是紧急集合的号令

无论何时

无论何地

都将勇往直前

无怨无悔

With no turning back.

Comrade in arm

Is a horse that gallops on the grassland.

It's a dragon swimming in the deep sea,

It's a tiger running down the mountain,

It's an eagle soaring in the sky,

It's a dove of peace in the global village,

It's a guard of the People's Republic.

Comrade in arm, my dear comrade in arm,

This sacred name

Is our common name.

It's the pursuit in our life.

We have forged the steel—like belief,

We hold the world in awe,

With firm and unyielding character.

义无反顾

战友

是奔驰在草原的骏马
是遨游在深海的蛟龙
是腾空在山崖的猛虎
是展翅在苍穹的雄鹰
是地球村的和平鸽
是共和国的守护神
战友啊战友
这个神圣的称呼
是我们共同的名字
是我们一生的追寻
铸就的钢铁信念
威震四海
铁骨铮铮

A Reunion of Veterans

Our voice was as loud as the gunfire in the firing range,
Liquor moistened our throats,
Veterans can't stop laughing when they recalled all this.
Even the yellow wine couldn't keep us from ignorantly joining the army.
Only those whom we called brothers shared our extreme grief,
Even beer couldn't cover the bubbles of the hard years.
A cup of tea was related to a foul wind and a rain of blood,
In exchange, the army song was loud and clear.

Changing clothes in tank trains,
It took us two days and three nights
To turn farmland into an airport runway.
Our baby faces
Were stamped with the vicissitudes of the years.
We ate the pig's feet horizontally and the corn vertically,
We caught frogs,
We played mahjong secretly,

老兵聚会

嗓门高得似靶场的炮声
烧酒润着喉咙
老兵一回忆就裹不住笑声
黄酒也拦不住入伍时的懵懂
肝肠寸断的只有唤作战友的兄弟
啤酒也遮不去困苦年月的气泡
一杯茶里的血雨腥风
换来军歌嘹亮

在闷罐火车的专列里换装
从农田到机场跑道
用了两天三夜的时光
曾经的娃娃脸上
印满了岁月沧桑
猪蹄横着咬,玉米直着啃
抓着蛙,麻将偷偷摸摸地输

We played ping-pong openly,

The roar on the basketball court was loud and clear.

The guitar was played with panache,

Harmonica sound conveyed homesickness.

From schoolchildren to soldiers of steel,

The majestic stride

Was made in the body from sunrise to sunset.

Even now talking about walking and wellness,

Little grandchildren and daughters' sons,

Has become frequent topic,

If you light us with alcohol,

You can still see

The grace of us standing inside the cabin of on the plane,

The fantasies of our youth,

The impulses in our blood.

In the course of the years,

With the elapse of forty years,

In the waves of time,

We have become grandfather and maternal grandfather,

And known how to go with the waves and how to go with the current,

A group of right arms were raised,

乒乓大大方方地打

篮球场上的吼声震天响

吉他表演着潇洒

口琴声传递着想家

从学生娃娃到铁血军人

那雄壮的步伐

在身体里行走,从日出到日落

即使如今谈走路聊养生

小孙子小外甥

变成了挂在嘴边的家常话

如果用酒精去点燃

你们依然能看到

我们站在飞机上的风采

年轻时的幻想

血液里的冲动

在岁月的长河里

四十年

我们已经在浪花里

做了爷爷成了外公

怎样地随波如何地逐流

一群右臂扬起

Five fingers held together as high as the eyebrows,

Ready to pay tribute to the former fame.

We once soared in the blue sky,

We once used armored vehicles,

We refused to put it down for a long time.

五指并拢与眉同高的手
随时准备致敬那曾经的芳华
曾经的蓝天翱翔
曾经的铁甲雄风
且久久不肯放下

Revisit Yang Village

Whenever I gaze at

The white clouds in the sky,

I seem to see

Airplanes flying in a cloudless sky.

Whenever I look at

The green mountains,

I seem to see

My comrades in arms.

Whenever I listen to

The rain and the wind,

In my ears echo

The loud and clear trumpet.

Over the past decades,

I crossed many waters;

Over the past decades,

I climbed many peaks,

Though stretching in my heart

再回杨村

每当我凝望
天上的白云
眼前便浮现
飞机遨翔蓝天
每当我注视
大山翠色
眼前会跃出
战友的身影
每当我谛听
雨打风鸣
耳畔会回响
嘹亮的号声

几十年
涉过多少水
几十年
踏过多少峰
心头伸展的

Are still

The flat airport runways;

What stand proudly in my heart

Are still

The fighting eagles.

Ah, the former

Airmen

Struggled here

Through cold

And heat.

Early in the morning,

We were first to cook.

At night,

We walked back to the barracks under the moon.

We "invited" the hares,

We "scattered" the birds.

We "troubleshooted" under the stars,

We "tested engines" under the moon.

We gave the fighting eagles a check—up,

We cleaned the fighting eagles.

We delivered the dawn hand in hand.

Black leather jackets

还是

机场跑道的一马平川

心中傲立的

还是

一架架战鹰

啊,曾经的

～～航空兵

在这里奋斗

冷风雪月

酷暑高温

清晨

我们升起第一缕炊烟

夜里

我们踏着月亮走回营门

我们"请"来野兔

我们"哄"走鸟群

我们披着星星"排故"

我们顶着月亮"试车"

我们给战鹰体检

我们给战鹰净身

我们手牵着手接生黎明

黑皮啊

Were worn until they were worn.

Poplars

Grew year after year.

Following decades of rain and wind,

Today I revisit Yang Village.

The wind is chanting, the clouds are surging,

To the sound of military trumpets, comrades in arms have a reunion.

In front of me are still what I remembered:

The proud persons in helmets

Fly the fighting eagles with proud

Across the sky.

Brothers in black leather jackets

Stand by the cabin in the wind.

The sunlight flashes on the planes,

Dew drops slide on the grass leaves.

The poplars are still standing tall,

The five−needle pines are still so green.

The sky is as blue as ever,

The clouds are still as white as ever,

The water is still as lucid as ever

Only gone are

穿了,再穿

白杨树

绿了,又绿

几十年雨啊几十年风

今天再回杨村

风来诵,云在涌

军号声声,战友重逢

眼前还是那记忆的画屏

戴上头盔的骄子

神气地驾着战鹰

威武长空

穿着黑皮的兄弟

站在机舱边临风

阳光在飞机上打闪

露珠在草叶上滑动

白杨树还是那么挺拔

五针松还是那么翠绿

天还是那么蓝

云还是那么白

水还是那么清

只是不见了

The old barracks,

Only gone are

The fighting eagles I used to maintain.

I am dying to take the instrument

To give the new jets a check—up.

How I would like to

Be a mechanic soldier again

In a black leather jacket in the moonlit night!

How I would like to step into

The door of the instructor team!

How I would like to

Heat up the stove in a snowy night,

Drink a bowl of hot soup,

And shabu—shabu a meal of cabbage!

How I would like to

Help new comrades with their lapel pins!

How I would like to

Present a recitation at a class meeting!

How I would like to once again

Call for the dawn!

How I would like to once again

Pilot the fighting eagle!

老式营房
只是不见了
我曾维护的战鹰

多想拿着仪器
给新机型做一次体检
多想在月夜
穿着黑皮
再当一次机务兵
多想再迈进
教导队的大门
多想在风雪之夜
烧热取暖的炉子
喝一碗热汤
涮一顿白菜
多想为新战友
缀一次领章
多想在班务会上
作一次朗诵
多想再一次
呼唤黎明
多想再一次
手牵着战鹰

Ah, all this has turned into

The unstoppable tide of Qiantang

And integrated into

The waves of the market economy.

It seems to be lost

Without a trace.

Ah, the tide is flashing on the horizon

A dazzling luster,

The waves are announcing

The march of the times.

Listen, in the distance comes

Heavenly sound,

The mountains and rivers

Are responding.

Our youth

Was dedicated to Yang Village

And to the airmen.

(Yang Village is an Air base of the PLA.)

啊,这一切已化作

挡不住的钱塘潮涌

已经融入

市场经济的波涛之中

似乎散失得

无影无踪

啊,潮涌在天际闪现

耀眼的光彩

波涛在告示

时代前进的脚步

听,远处传来

一声声天籁

山山水水

都在回应

我们的青春

献给了杨村

献给了航空兵

(杨村,是中国人民解放军空军八一飞行表演队驻地。)

I'm Proud of My Youth

Unknowingly, my temples have turned gray,
I often recall the most beautiful feelings of my youth.
Smooth runways of the airport
Was accompanied by the ideal of loving the sapphire sky of the motherland,
Waiting for the return of the fighting eagles on a mission,
I didn't care about the fatigue in oil-stained uniform,
Nor did I care about the sleepiness during continuous flights.
In the summer heat, I had three meals a day
With the runway as the table; it didn't matter if it tasted good or not.
In the winter cold, working late into the night,
With the fighting eagles as my partners, it didn't matter if it was chilly.

I can't forget that when it was more than 10 degrees below zero,
I crawled into the narrow air flue in thin clothes.

为青春骄傲

不知不觉两鬓已经斑白
常忆起青春时最美的情怀
一马平川的机场跑道
伴着"我爱祖国蓝天"的理想
等待着执行任务的战鹰返航
不在乎油渍满身的疲惫
不计较连续飞行的困乏
夏日酷暑,一日三餐
以跑道为桌,有味无味无所谓
冬日严寒,披星戴月
以战鹰为伍,冷乎冻乎不在乎

忘不了,零下十几度
单衣薄衫爬进狭窄的进气道

I can't forget that during troubleshooting at night,
The lieutenant fell off the wing of the plane.
I can't forget that during windstorms and sandstorms,
We got heavily dusty either in the morning or in the afternoon.
I can't forget when I suffered headache from a cold,
The instructor sent me meals with eggs reserved for the sick.
I can't forget in the training field,
The sound of shouting and yelling was brimmed with determination.
I can't forget after flights,
Our expenienced regimental commander made serious and severe criticisms.
I can't forget during the military parades,
The vigorous posture and loud slogans demonstrated our might.

The bitter north wind blew relentlessly,
Making mountains barren and breaking tree branches,
But stopping short of ruining the green dream of the young soldiers.
The scorching sun burns cruelly,

忘不了,故障不过夜

从机翼上摔下来的中队长

忘不了,劲风扬沙

一天四两土上午不够下午补的味道

忘不了,头痛感冒

指导员送来盖着鸡蛋的病号饭

忘不了,训练场上

叫声吼声呼喊声血气方刚

忘不了,飞行结束后

讲评时严肃又严厉的老团长

忘不了,阅兵式时

矫健的身姿响亮的口号威武雄壮

凛冽的北风,无情地吹过

吹秃了荒山,吹折了树枝

却吹不动戍边少年的绿色梦想

炎炎的烈日,残忍地燃烧

Burning the aircraft skin and keeping the birds away,
But stopping short of ruining the loyalty of young soldiers to the fighting eagles.
Now we have taken off our uniforms,
But the iron bones forged in the military
Still stand out in the market economy.
Although we have left the army barracks,
The rock—firm temperament shaped in the military
Still prevails in every kind of competition.

Every time we have a reunion of comrades in arms, we still talk about
The old stories even since we first joined the army.
Every time we talk to each other on the phone, we think about
The former soldiers and commanders.
Every time we talk to each other, we still discuss
The pursuits and aspirations in the era of our youthhood.
In rains and winds, the loud and clear sound of the bugle echoes in my ears,
Amidst engine sounds, I miss the fighting eagles I once maintained.

烧烫了飞机蒙皮,烧跑了小鸟
却烧不走青年军人对战鹰的忠诚
如今我们已经脱下了军装
但军营里铸就的铮铮铁骨
依然昂扬于市场经济大潮
虽然我们已经离开了军营
但军营里塑造的磐石性情
依然跃马剑气于百舸争流

每一次战友相聚,念叨的
还是刚入伍时的那些陈年旧事
每一次战友通话,牵挂的
还是曾经的战友和首长
每一次战友聊天,交流的
还是年轻时的追求和向往
雨打风鸣,耳畔便回响嘹亮的号声
引擎鸣响,心中便惦记曾经维护的战鹰

绿色军营,遗落了我们的所有青春
漫长跑道,洒满了我们的最美阳光
我骄傲,我是共和国的航空兵
我骄傲,我是新时代的中国军人

The green barracks are where all our youth was left behind,
The long runway is filled with our most beautiful sunshine.
I am proud to be an airman of the PRC,
I am proud to be a Chinese soldier of the new era.

Your Silhouette in Charging

You are running, you are charging,
You choose to go forward.
You step on the earth shaking under the aftershock,
You brave the falling stones and dust of the collapse,
Leaving us a silhouette of you in dashing.

At this moment, you no longer care about
What kind of danger you will encounter,
Even your young life which can be swallowed up by the mountain.
You keep running as long as women, senior citizens
And the people are in distress.
This is the call to charge,
This is the order to advance.

Run, run,
Dash toward the dangerous place.
Your camouflage is covered with the dust of war,
Which must definitely be

奔跑的背影

你在奔跑,你在冲锋
你选择了勇往直前
你踏着余震下的地动山摇
你迎着塌方的陨石和灰尘
你留给我们奔跑的背影

此刻,你已顾不上
自己会遇到怎样的险情
甚至被大山吞噬掉年轻的生命
只要前面还有姐妹,还有老人
还有咱们老百姓
这就是冲锋的号角
这就是前进的命令

奔跑,奔跑
向着危险的地方奔跑
你一身布满征尘的迷彩
一定是,一定是

The most touching scenery.

You leave the hope of life to others,

You take the threat of death very lightly.

You are also the apple of your parents' eye,

You are also the backbone of your wife and children.

But at such a time

You cannot care about the hope and advice of your loved ones.

In a time of crisis, as a soldier

You step forward in face of danger.

The view of the back of your running and your camouflage

Touches hundreds of millions of people

In today's China.

You are a hero,

But you say you are not as good as a hero,

And that staying loyal to the motherland and the people,

Is the honorable mission of every soldier.

At the moment when the sky were falling and the earth were collapsing,

The view of the back of your running

最最感动人心的风景
你把生的希望,留给别人
把死神的威胁,看得很淡很轻

你也是父母的心头肉
你也是妻儿的顶梁柱
可这样的时刻
你顾不上亲人的盼望和叮咛
危难关头,以一名战士的身份
迎着危难前行

你奔跑的背影,你一身的迷彩
在今天的中华大地
已经感动了亿万民众
你是英雄
可你说,我们算不上英雄
忠于祖国,忠于人民
是每个战士光荣的使命

在天塌地陷的时刻
你奔跑的背影

Demonstrates you are stalwart and brave,
Strong and firm.
With you there, the people
Feel assured and warm.
With your protection, the people
Feel comforted and peaceful.

Salute! The view of the back of your running,
Salute! The people's soldier.

On the night of August 12, 2017, Shanghai
(On the night of August 12, 2017, in its Network News Broadcast program, CCTV reported the abovementioned soldier in the Jiuzhaigou earthquake rescue. Moved and emotional, I wrote this poem in his honor.)

刚毅,勇敢

伟岸,坚定

有你们在,百姓的心头

就觉得踏实,觉得温暖

有你们护佑,人民群众

就倍感欣慰,倍感安宁

敬礼！奔跑的背影

敬礼！人民子弟兵

2017年8月12日夜,于上海

(2017年8月12日夜,央视《新闻联播》报道中有一张九寨沟地震救援中的战士的照片,感动、感慨之余,以诗为证。)

Salute! I Do Not Want to Disturb You
A visit to the "Air Force Wall of Heroes"

Salute! I do not want to disturb you.
This azure sky is so peaceful.
I look at you silently in front of the Wall of Heroes.
I know that what is engraved on the wall is only a miniature of life,
But each name represents a body that will never fall.

Salute! I do not want to disturb you.
This black land is so quiet.
I hold you tightly in my arms in front of the Wall of Heroes.
I know you can no longer understand the depth of love,
But you are not a bit sad and distant.

Salute! I do not want to disturb you.
This wall stained with blood is so quiet.
I miss you so much in front of the Wall of Heroes.
I know you can no longer feel the love of your comrades in arms,

敬礼！我不惊扰你
——参观"空军英雄墙"而作

敬礼！我不惊扰你
这片湛蓝的天空是这样安宁
英雄墙前我默默地注视着你
我知道刻在墙上的只是生命的缩影
但每一个名字都是永远不倒的身躯

敬礼！我不惊扰你
这片黑色的土地是这样安静
英雄墙前我紧紧地拥抱着你
我知道你已经无法体会爱的深沉
但你却没有一点忧伤和疏离

敬礼！我不惊扰你
这片用鲜血染红的墙壁是这样肃静
英雄墙前我深深地思念着你
我知道你已经不能感受战友情深

But you were so brave for the sake of the country's peace.

Salute! I do not want to disturb you.
This wall of heroic souls is so peaceful.
My heart calls out to you in front of the Wall of Heroes.
I know that although we can no longer fly in formation,
But the love for the azure sky of our country is eternal in our hearts.

Salute! I do not want to disturb you.
This warm and just wall is so magnificent.
In front of the Wall of Heroes, I guard you with the highest respect.
I know you will never be able to see it in person again,
But the monument of history will always bear the mark of your greatness.

Salute! I do not worry about you.
O, 1,776 great martyrs!
The motherland has not forgotten you, nor have the people.
You are the most eternal memory of the People's Air Force.
Salute, I do not want to disturb you; we do not want to disturb you...

但为了国家安宁你是那样英勇无比

敬礼！我不惊扰你
这片英魂铸就的墙壁是这样宁静
英雄墙前我的心在呼唤着你
我知道尽管我们再也不能编队飞行
但对祖国蓝天的眷恋是心中的永恒

敬礼！我不惊扰你
这片和煦正义的墙壁是这样壮丽
英雄墙前我用最崇高的敬意守护着你
我知道你再也不能亲临其境
但历史的丰碑永远铭刻着你的伟绩

敬礼！我不惊忧你
1776位伟大的英烈啊！
祖国没有忘记你，人民没有忘记你
你们是人民空军最永恒的惦记
敬礼，我不惊扰你，我们不惊扰你……

The Moon Is a Faint Nostalgia

The moon is a faint nostalgia.
No matter where you go,
It illuminates every inch of skin.
O nostalgia,
It's not a small postage stamp,
Nor is it a shallow Strait.
It's a longing in my heart.
The longing is round,
It is round for wine—the Gu Yue Long Shan of my hometown;
The longing is thin,
It is thin for Lanting, a thousand years of legend.

Thousands of years of vicissitudes, long thoughts of autumn,
The romance winding on both sides of the Grand Canal.
From Chang'an to South of the Yangtze River,
From South of the Yangtze River to Zhedong,
Crossing the earthly smoke and rain,

月亮是淡淡的乡愁

月亮是淡淡的乡愁
无论走到哪里
都将每一寸肌肤照亮
乡愁啊
已经不是一张小小的邮票
也不是一湾浅浅的海峡
而是一怀相思在心头
相思圆了
圆在酒中就是家乡的"古越龙山"
相思瘦了
瘦在兰亭就是传神的千古风流

千年沧桑,秋思悠悠
蜿蜒在大运河两岸的浪漫
从长安到江南
从江南到浙东
穿越尘世烟雨

Taking a curtain of moonlight to Kuaiji.

Set up a table for poetry,

Invite the Sage of Calligraphy Wang Xizhi for a drink.

Invite Xu Wei to the banquet,

Enjoy the fragrance of orange osmanths with amid writing poems and painting.

The moonlight with love

Has fascinated so many ancestors and mortals.

Tonight, let's have a drink together,

No matter how many we will be, including my shadow.

As long as we drink it all, we will have a great feeling.

Taking advantage of the light of the shadows,

Bite into a moonlit haze.

Pillowed by the softness of Jian Lake,

Wait for a night.

Remember the full moon in my hometown,

Remember the faint nostalgia.

牵一帘月色到会稽
摆上一桌诗会
邀书圣羲之品酒
请青藤老人入宴
吟诗作画，赏丹桂飘香

多情的月光啊
曾经醉了多少先祖凡人
今夜，让我们也来一次对饮
不管对影成几人
只要一饮而尽，就有一番豪情
趁着这影子的光芒
咬一个月色朦胧
枕鉴湖水的柔情
静候一夜的光阴
记住故乡的满月
记住淡淡的乡愁

Everlasting Nostalgia
In Memory of Yu Kwang-chung

You departed your life,

You really met your end,

In a rainy, wet and cold winter.

With 70−year,

Three−generation,

Thick nostalgia,

You went to your last resting place

On the other side of the Strait.

Grandpa said,

The other side of the sea

Was his nostalgia.

At that time,

A small postage stamp

Sent back

Infinite love for each other

And Endless sorrow.

Dad said,

永远的乡愁
——纪念余光中

您走了
您真的走了
在一个阴雨湿冷的冬天
带着七十载
带着三代人
浓浓的乡愁
陨落在
海峡的那一头

爷爷说
海的那头
是他的乡愁
那个时候呀
一枚小小的邮票
寄回了
无限的相思
无尽的哀愁

爸爸说

The small grave

Was his nostalgia.

Grandma was inside of it,

He was outside of it.

He buried his love for her

In his heart.

Tonight,

You

Crossed the great divide.

The wind, cold and swishing,

Can't blow away

Your nostalgia of seventy years.

Rain, drifting and sprinkling,

Falling down

As long sadness.

I ask the fallen leaves

Where you went?

The fallen leaves say,

We return to our roots.

You went

Where there is nostalgia.

矮矮的坟墓
是他的乡愁
奶奶在里头
他在外头
他把相思
埋在了心里头

今夜呀
您却自己
走在了前头
风,冷嗖嗖
吹不尽
七十载的乡愁
雨,飘飘洒洒
落下的
是长长的伤感

我问落叶
您去了哪里
落叶说
落叶归根呀
哪里有乡愁
您就去了哪里

Over and over again,

I read your nostalgia.

I felt like I could see

On the other side of the sea,

Sitting on an old chair,

The old man with a pair of gold-rimmed glasses

had really been lost.

I asked the sound of the waves

Where you had gone?

The waves were rolling in

To the eastern shore.

I touched the wet shore,

The shore was still

Quietly waiting.

I look away, I look away at

The shallow strait,

Feelings of my love

Rush in my heart.

From this end to the other end,

You spent your whole life

Just to feel the warmth of home.

我一遍又一遍
读着您的乡愁
仿佛看到了
海的那边
坐在老旧的椅子上
架着一副金丝眼镜的老人
真的已经走在了前头

我问涛声
您去了哪里
波涛滚滚而来
拍向东边的岸
我抚摸着潮湿的岸
岸依然在
静静地守候

我遥望,遥望那
浅浅的海峡
一怀相思
涌在心头
从这头,到那头
您用尽一生
只想感受家的温暖

Mother's Hands

Mother's hands,
They used to be so dexterous,
Stitch by stitch
Mending my childhood.
With a pair of new, strong shoes every year,
With new homemade clothes every season,
Wearing a threaded scarf knitted by my mother,
I stood out among my classmates.
The little deer embroidered on the chest of my white shirt
Was all the happy memory of my childhood.

Later on,
Mother made a big red flower with her own hands,
And hung it on my chest.
With best wishes, she sent me onto
The train to the army barracks.
In the spring of that year,
Mother put away the clothes I left
Decently in a case.

母亲的手

母亲的手
曾经是那样灵巧
一针一线
缝补着我的童年
一年有一双结实的新鞋
一季有一季自制的新衣
围上一条母亲织的线围脖
变成了同学中的风流小生
绣在白衬衣胸前的那只小鹿
是我所有童年的快乐记忆

后来呀
母亲亲手做了一朵大红花
挂在了我的胸前
叮嘱着将我送上了
开往军营的列车
就在那一年春天
母亲将我留下的衣服
方方正正存放在一个箱子里

Then every winter
She put her hand-made shoe soles
Neatly on my bedside.
Mother said,
Behave decently,
Behave neatly.

Nowadays my mothers' fingers
Have bent and deformed,
Which can no longer squeeze tightly
The needle she has been using all her life.
The squinted eyes behind a pair of presbyopic glasses
Lack the look I am familiar with,
But demonstrate more peace and tranquility.
Her chatter
Is refreshing, sweet and nourishing
Like the milk candy she fed me when I was a child.

Time flies.
Mother's trembling fingers
Still squeeze the needle and thread through her white hair,
Sewing the warm and quiet time,
Can't mend the vicissitude of the years.

然后在每一年冬季
将亲手纳的鞋底
整整齐齐放在我的床头
母亲说：
做人就要整整齐齐
方方正正

现在的母亲啊
手指已经弯曲变形
已经捏不紧
那根捏了一辈子的针
花镜背后眯起的眼睛
也少了我熟悉的神
却多了安详与宁静
她的唠叨哟
犹如儿时塞在我小嘴里的奶糖
浑身清爽，甜蜜滋润

岁月悠悠，弹指一瞬
母亲颤颤巍巍的手指
依然捏着针线在白发里穿行
缝制着温暖恬静的时光
却修补不了沧桑岁月的年轮

Don't Leave Me More With Memories

Don't leave me with more memories.

The life of a person is long yet short,

It's so short that before you begin to enjoy the beautiful time

You are already in your late years.

In the days of life and death,

Dying words can't express the full meaning.

O, you! My dear father.

When you were young, you fought before the founding of the PRC.

All the cells in your body

Left only the instinct to survive.

You seemed to have forgotten the wisdom that belongs to you

And the joy and innocence that you should have.

When you were young, you kept faith in your heart,

The blush of the sun had smoothed out the suffering.

A new life started with the birth of the new republic,

不要留给我更多的回忆

不要留给我更多的回忆
人的一生很长且又很短
短得来不及享用美好年华
就已经身处迟暮
在生与死相伴的时日里
弥留的话无法表达意思的完整

您啊！我亲爱的父亲
年少时，在旧社会里抗争
身体里的所有细胞
只留下了生存的本能
似乎忘却了属于自己的智慧
以及，本该有的快乐和童真

青春时，将信念装进心里
红色的太阳已将苦难抹平
新的人生随民族的起来而开启

You were loyal to the oath you took with your right hand raised.
Entering school, you studied hard for medical knowledge,
At the grassroots, you competed for the first place.

In the age of maturity, you fought the storm with a big flag.
Coming from deep in the mountains in the hometown of Xishi,
You approached the romantic beauty of Hangzhou.
Your solid footprints spread across the land of eastern Zhejiang
Camping on the Lanting River and Ruoye Creek to wipe out schistosomiasis.
But your life was quietly taken away by schistosomiasis.

Do not leave me more memories,
Don't stand on the high ground of life's sorrow,
Work into the dark night for the beginning of life.
Summarize the spiritual core of the vicissitudes of life.
For death, I will not curse with tears;
I can only resent the merciless passing of time.

(Written in memory of my father on the Tomb-Sweeping Festival)

忠诚履行举起右手时的誓言
进校门,努力苦读医学知识
下基层,参加竞赛勇争第一

成熟的年代里,扛大旗战风云
从西施故里的大山深处而来
走进西子湖畔的浪漫美丽
坚实的足迹遍及浙东大地
宿营兰亭江、若耶溪送走瘟神
自己却被瘟神悄悄夺走生命

不要留给我更多的回忆
不要站在生命悲哀的高处
走进人生大幕拉起的暗夜
总结沧桑岁月的精神内核
对于死亡,我不会用热泪去诅咒
只能怨恨,怨恨光阴无情地消逝

(清明节,纪念父亲而作)

Seeking Dreams

In memory of my father

Who can know the pain you endured from a long illness?
You were exhausted all over with a thin and bony body.
The sympathy of neighbors was only a sigh.
Having a strange occupational disease, you had no more desire,
Only panic and pity.

With anxiety and fear, I was powerless to fight,
Who would like to smell the strange odor of antiseptic solution?
I saw all kinds of medical tubes and all kinds of medical fluids.
The white space had horrible images,
I couldn't get away from the fading shadowless lights.

As your son, I couldn't stop the pillar from falling apart.
Against my will, everything came to an end,

寻 梦
——追忆父亲

谁能知晓,久病不愈的苦痛
拖着一身疲惫,瘦骨嶙峋
邻居的同情心,只是一声声叹息
得了职业怪病,没有了欲望
只有惊恐和悲悯

焦虑和恐惧,我无力抗争
谁会喜欢闻着消毒药水的怪味
各式管子,各种液体
白色的空间里,画面恐怖
无法脱离,渐识渐远的无影灯

儿子的责任,扛不住栋梁塌落
痛恨何用,幕落曲终

沙漏的宿命,终将见底告罄
我无力再继续陪伴您的苦痛
最终的结果依然冷酷无情

七十四岁呀,毕竟还算年轻
可怕的夜色,为何选择此刻剧终
大幕拉起,我却依旧苦等
冬至或者清明,在每一个节日里
我会沿着您远去的方向,寻梦

Like the sands through the hourglass.
I could no longer accompany you in your pain,
The final result was still cold and heartless.

At seventy-four, you were still young.
Why did the terrible night choose this moment to end?
The curtain rose, but I was still waiting.
During the winter solstice and the Tomb-Sweeping Festival,
I'll follow the direction you went in seeking dreams.

Father's Feet

I often think of father's swollen feet,

No shoes fitted them.

You couldn't support your wobbly body,

You groaned in pain even when the clear river reflected the bright moon,

You remained drowsy with sleep when the sunlight shined into the balcony.

In the blink of an eye, you fell asleep in the rocking chair.

Looking at your swollen feet cleaned with water,

Night after night, you rubbed the sore spots.

Like touching something dear to you,

You gently rubbed with a hot towel over your limp body.

You used to be a man who stood on the top of the mountain,

With three children who hailed you as Mr. Wonderful.

I recall the man who, dressed in a sports outfit after dinner,

父亲的双脚

常常想起那双浮肿的脚
已经找不到合适的鞋
摇摇晃晃的身体如何支撑
清清河水映照明月时的呻吟
阳光射进阳台依然睡意昏沉

眨眼间,就在摇椅上睡着
看着被水洗净鼓鼓的这双脚
夜复一夜,揉搓着疼痛之处
就像抚摸自己的亲爱之物
用热毛巾轻轻擦过瘫软的身体

曾经是站立山顶的男子汉
膝下三个子女捧其为男神
想起那个晚餐后一身运动装

Competed in the basketball court with the nickname "Tank".
As a child, I saw you climbing trees with your bare hands,
Standing high with your eyes on the road ahead.

In the special era,
You measured a section of history with your feet,
You stood firm with courage by a tablet,
Copying "Schistosomiasis must be eradicated",
Stopping the national treasure from being removed.
Since then, the tablet from our forefathers has always stood tall.

What kind of memories will remain in the world?
Drifting in the air are snowflakes,
Or it could also be flying dust.
When I found your supporting feet,
They were as warm as a hand under the warm winter sun.
Every step you took was down−to−earth,
There was always a path shining from beneath your feet.

驰骋在篮球场上的外号坦克
我童年时看到徒手攀爬大树的男人
站在高处目光投向前方的路

在那个特殊的时代里
您的双脚丈量着一段历史
用勇气站稳在一块碑旁
抄写"一定要消灭血吸虫病"
国宝级的御碑才没被搬移
从此先祖的碑文始终昂然屹立

有什么样的记忆,会在世间留存
飘荡在空气中的是雪花
或许,是飞舞的尘埃
当我找到那双脚,支撑着
就像冬日暖阳里的手一样温暖
走过的每一步都是踏实的
都有道路从脚下闪亮着出现

Yearning

I want to go back to my hometown in the countryside and build a big house,
There is a river in front of the house and a mountain behind it.
The house is surrounded by a garden,
I also want to is planted with some flowers and vegetables,
Including my favorite white magnolia.
And plant two types of osmanthus trees and red yew trees.
On the hill behind the house,
There are botanicals, chestnuts and bamboos.
In the river in front of the house,
There are fish, shrimps, and Xishi washing clothes.

This big house
Must be able to accommodate my childhood, my nostalgia
There is a large study room,
Large enough for the Twenty-Four Histories,
For the Dream of the Red Chamber,
For Laozi, Confucius and Zhuangzi,

向 往

我想回乡下老家建一栋大房子
房前有条河,屋后有座山
房子被一个园子包围着
种一些花草和蔬菜
还有我喜欢的白玉兰
再种两棵桂花树和红豆杉
屋后的山上
有香榧、板栗、竹子
房前的河里
有鱼、有虾、有浣纱

这栋大房子
要能包容我的童年,我的乡愁
有个大大的书房
装得下二十四史
装得下红楼寻梦
装得下老子、孔子和庄子

For the history of world civilization,

For the remaining two thirds of my life.

In this big house,

I want the four generations of my family to live together.

I want to play hide—and—seek with the little kids,

So they can't find where I am.

A big dining table,

Big enough for my relatives from the countryside,

For my colleagues from the city, for my former comrades in arms.

This big house

Can keep my lifelong emotions stable,

Can accept my lifetime memories.

I want to enjoy the warmth in enough space,

I want to age slowly in enough space.

I believe that this big house's

Plan is in my mind,

And its ownership certificate is in my heart.

装得下世界文明史
装得下我三分之二的余生

这栋大房子
我要儿孙绕膝四世同堂
我要与小家伙们捉迷藏
叫他们找不到我在哪里
一个大餐桌
坐得下乡下老家的亲戚
城里的同事,曾经的战友

这栋大房子
能把握住我一生的情绪
能接受我一辈子的回忆
我要在足够的空间里享受温暖
我要在足够的空间里慢慢衰老
我相信,这栋大房子
图纸,在我的脑海里
产证,在我的心坎里

Father's River

The sinuating and twisting Puyang River
Comes from the hometown I miss too much.
It's the river where Xishi washed clothes and fascinated fish,
It records the rise and fall of the Spring and Autumn Period.
It records the peace and tranquility of the ancient State of Yue.
It's my father's river.
It is as brave as my father,
It is as open-minded as my father.

Father and the Puyang River have merged into one.
For more than 3,000 days and nights,
In the land of my hometown,
I watched over the Puyang River like I did over my father.
My father has gone to the ocean with the river,
My love for him flowed far away with the river.
My father's river is so long,
My missing are so far away.

父亲的江

蜿蜒曲折的浦阳江
来自魂牵梦绕的故乡
那是西施浣纱沉鱼之江
记录着春秋时期兴衰存亡
记载着古代越国和平安详
那是一条父亲的江
他像父亲那样勇敢
他像父亲那样豁达

父亲与浦阳江已融为一体
三千多个日日夜夜
在故乡的土地上
我守着浦阳江像守着父亲
而父亲已随江水奔向了大海
我的牵挂随江水流向了远方
父亲的江那么那么长
我的思念那么那么远

My Daughter Is Wearing a Doctoral Mortarboard

Second by second, minute by minute,

My daughter grew up for twenty—eight years.

Inch by inch, foot by foot,

You crossed the vast Pacific Ocean.

Beginning with horizontal, vertical and falling strokes,

You accomplished your highest academic ideal.

Under the doctoral mortarboard,

Your young and childlike face

Reveals a bit of literary character,

Assumes bit of aura,

Adds a little freshness,

Appears to be charming.

Behind the beautiful myopic glasses,

Your eyes shine with confidence and determination.

女儿戴上了博士帽

一秒一分一刻
成长了二十八个春秋
一寸一尺一丈
跨越了万里太平洋
一横一竖一捺
成就了最优秀的学习理想

博士帽下
那张稚嫩清秀的脸
透出了几分文艺
跃上了几分灵气
增添了几分清新
画出了几分妩媚
秀气的近视眼镜背后
闪烁着自信和坚定的眼神

It Sounds as if My Daughter Is Calling Me

Every time I hear

A little girl calls out "Daddy, Daddy",

The tender and clear voice

Would freeze my footsteps.

I look back and look for

The familiar voice in the crowd,

But, every time I look

I feel a sense of loss in my heart.

Every time I stare

A look of disappointment would appear on my face.

I pull myself together,

Collecting my thoughts,

Then I suddenly remember

My own baby...

Has grown up.

仿佛是女儿在叫我

每一次耳边传来
小女孩叫"爸爸、爸爸"
稚嫩又清脆的声音
都会凝固住自己的脚步
回头凝神寻找,寻找
人群中那熟悉的叫声
可是,每一次寻找
我的内心都会有一阵失落
每一回凝望
脸上就会写满失望的表情
我定一定自己的眼睛
缓一缓自己的神
才忽然想起
自己的宝贝——
已经长大成人

The Unknown

I don't know
From which day
You have been holding my hand like this,
Follow me slowly and shakily.

I don't know
How to describe
Your tender little hands
wrapped around my shoulders and led me on the bike.

I don't know
In which photo that was taken,
The small flowers on the roadside recorded
The streets you took me through.

I don't know
The way you moved your hand and the way you walked
Was like a world coming to me,
I loved you so much that I took them all.

不知道

不知道
应该从哪一天算起
你这样牵着我的手
摇摇晃晃慢慢跟着我走

不知道
应该如何来描述
你那双细嫩的小手
搂着我的肩 带着我骑上了单车

不知道
拍摄的哪一张照片里
路边的小花记录下
你带着我经过的那些街口

不知道
你的一举手一投足
像一个世界向我走来
我爱意昭昭，一一认领

I don't know

All the things with slow steps that fall are so light

A dandelion seed

Falls like a parachute, sprouting and maturing.

I don't know

In your growth,

Whether your youth is closer

or my youth is farther away.

不知道

所有落下的慢事物是那么轻

一颗蒲公英的种子

降落伞般地落下、发芽、成熟

不知道

在你的成长里

是你的青春近了一些

还是我的青春远了一些

The Days of Fantasy
Written on June 1st Children's Day

Childhood

Burns an ordinary day

And makes it blazing hot.

From the nursery rhyme "I found a penny on the road"

to wearing the red scarf,

We are the "successors of communism".

The glowing dream

Still echoes on the pillow,

But the passion of the wind

Turned into disappearing white clouds.

Each cloud is where

My smiling face lives

And my moving—on back.

My soul will take root

Wherever the clouds fall.

After moving on for more than half of my life,

My innocence by nature remains.

幻想的日子
——写在"六一"儿童节

童年
将一个普通的日子
炙烤得炽热无比
从"我在马路边捡到一分钱"
到系上红领巾
我们是"共产主义接班人"
发着光热的梦幻
依稀还在枕边回响
但风的激情
却化作了飘逝的白云
每一朵云里
都住着我的笑脸
印着跋涉的背影
云朵落在哪里
我的灵魂就会在哪里落地生根
走了半生多
停不下来的还是那份纯真

Just like the wheels that race with you,

They bring rain and snow along

And washes away the wrinkles on your face.

Decades of vicissitudes,

Decades of struggles,

I remember a

Day full of fantasy:

"June 1st."

On this day we are the same:

"Listen,

It sounds like lipples of a river."

恰如与你赛跑的车轮

裹挟着雨雪

冲刷着脸上的皱纹

几十年沧桑

几十年拼争

记住了一个

充满着幻想的日子

"六一"

在这一天我们相同了

"你听——

它盛放的声音像河流"

Childhood

The sleepless night is noisy:
The red sweater knitted by mother,
Brother's well-fitting little army uniform,
Dad riding a bicycle whistling,
My Russian skates,
All come flashing like a slide show,
To the tune of the sound of cars passing by.

The white light from the projector
Lights up the joyful faces of my childhood.
In the summer, I opened my arms
Embracing the big poplar tree in front of the door.
How many little bird friends were hidden there?
I contacted them with my eyes,
I accompanied them with whispers.
Later on, they all flew away upwards.
All that fell in droves
Was like the ever-clean little flower on the dress of my sister who married far away.

童　年

无眠的夜是嘈杂的
妈妈织的红毛衣
弟弟合身的小军装
爸爸骑着"永久"吹着口哨
我的俄式溜冰鞋
和着汽车驶过的声音
幻灯片般一闪一闪而来

放映机投放出的白光
打亮了童年时常欢喜的脸
盛夏张开双臂
拥抱门前的大榕树
藏了多少知心的小鸟
我用目光联系过它们
用悄悄话陪伴过它们
后来,它们都向上飞走了
纷纷落下的
好似远嫁的姐姐连衣裙上
那朵耐脏的小花

You Are Like a Bright Star

In Celebration of the 50th birthday of my good buddy Shao Jun

You are like a bright star,

Transmitting the light of the international capital markets.

From the vast and boundless US dollar market

To the difficult development of RMB funds,

Your dazzling twinkle

Stimulates the changing soul of the capital markets.

You have awakened with wisdom

The desire and trust of investors.

Raise your glass! It's your birthday.

By UN standards,

You are still a young man.

Young and experienced,

That's great wealth and luck.

Listen, the waves of the Huangpu River are light tonight,

They're the happy applauses for your birthday.

Look, how soft the moonlight outside the window tonight,

你是一颗璀璨的星
——为好兄弟邵俊五十岁而作

你是一颗璀璨的星
传递着国际资本市场的光芒
从浩瀚无垠的美元市场
到艰难发展的人民币基金
你耀眼的闪烁
刺激着资本市场风云多变的灵魂
你用智慧唤醒了
投资人的渴望和信任

举杯吧!这是你的生日
按联合国标准
你还是一个青年人
年轻,有了经历
那是极大的富有和幸运
听,今晚黄浦江的波涛多么轻盈
那是为你的生日献上快乐的掌声
看,今夜窗外的月亮多么柔情

That's envious eyes for your birthday.

Your professionalism,
Your calm and steady character,
Act if you were a butler of the Prime Minister's official residence.
You can dispel the haze of confusion,
Ensuring the dawn of absolute sanctity escapes the darkness.
Here we are close to hope,
We are familiar with the true meaning of the capital markets.
We take comfort in this quiet night,
Gazing at our stars.

Sing! It's your birthday today.
Fifty years old! What a tempting age!
The curtain of life has just opened,
At this moment, you really know:
What loss is and what calmness is,
What generosity is and what broadmindedness is.
When you are in pain, you can give yourself a smile,
That is a kind of relief.

那是为你的生日奉上美慕的眼睛

你专业的素养
你沉稳的性格
像极了首相官邸的掌门人
能把迷离的阴霾驱散
让绝对神圣的黎明躲过黑暗
我们在这里贴近了希望
我们熟悉了资本市场的真谛
我们欣慰在这个宁静的夜晚
把我们的星星凝望

歌唱吧！这是你的生日
五十岁啊！多么诱人的年龄
人生的大幕刚刚开启
此刻，才真正懂得
什么是吃亏，什么是淡然
什么是大气，什么是达观
痛苦的时候，能给自己一个微笑
那是一种解脱

When you fail, you can give yourself a smile,

That is confidence.

Tonight, the applause of your fellows support your sincerity,

Tonight, the smiling faces of your fellows follow your determination.

You are the talented student of Fudan University,

You are the elite of Shanghai Jiaotong University.

You are the trendsetter of the market economy,

You are the navigator of the capital markets.

You are the real brave man,

You are like a shining star.

失败的时候,能给自己一个微笑

那是一份自信

今夜,朋友们的掌声支持着你的真诚

今夜,朋友们的笑脸追随着你的坚定

你是复旦的才子

你是交大的精英

你是市场经济的弄潮儿

你是资本市场的引航人

你是真正的勇者

你是一颗璀璨的星

Spring

The earth. Let the south wind blow through,
The swallows return,
And the shoots can be green.
Spring is like a drawn bow.

Reborn. Even if it comes without hope.
The water under the frozen surface of keep flowing,
Calycanthus praecox remains in the making following blossoms.
Spring, shooting down a field of surprises.

Birds perching on the branches. Fish swimming in clear waters.
Those past events that are linked by time,
Are silenced in the song of the time.
Longing for each other.
Spring, like an arrow shot without a trace.

春

大地。任南风吹过
燕子归来
嫩芽就可以绿了
春,是张开的弓

重生。即使不带着希望而来
冰封的河面下的流水依旧
蜡梅花开后还在酝酿
春,射落一地惊喜

栖鸟枝头。鱼翔浅底
那些用光阴串联的往事
沉寂于岁月的一曲
长相思
春,一箭漫漫无痕

Spring Snow

The sunshine takes off its warm clothes,
Drifting down in fine pieces.
This is the virtual language,
This is the charm from the bones,
Adorning
The early spring yet to become in full blossom;
Continuing
The firmness of the plum blossoms;
Falling on the fields with heads bowed;
Falling on the lonely streets and alleys.
Like a woman you love,
Inviting you to join the painting like an angel.
Ellipsis—like
Purity and flawlessness.
White and light,
Purifying the world;
Purifying the heart as well.

春 雪

阳光,脱下身上的暖衣
细碎地飘落
这是虚拟的语言
这是有骨骼的妩媚
装扮着
没来得及浓妆艳抹的初春
绵延着
金梅花开的坚定
落于低着头的田野
落于寂寞的街衢小径
宛如爱情中的如意女子
天使一般邀你入画
省略号般的
纯净无瑕
洁白轻盈
白了世界
也白了凡心

Beginning of Spring

Listen, the bursts of firecrackers,

with the steps of the old ox and the plow harrow,

Has sounded in the solid earth.

The early morning birds are making

The music that welcomes the triumph return of wild geese.

The silent sky, suppressed by the cold, suddenly

Resurrects the warm and sentimental feeling of d é j à vu.

The willow leaves by the river, shaking off the white frost,

Also shine with green in the sunlight,

Spread to the fish in the river

The message of finding partners and mating.

The moths that are ready to move quietly announce

The grand opening for seasonal reincarnation.

The air blows a warm coded signal

Reminding the people

Every hour that slips away

Has infinite vigor and is beautiful and young.

立 春

听,那一声声爆竹
携着老牛和犁耙的脚步
已经响起在坚实的大地
清晨的鸟儿,吹奏着
迎接大雁凯旋的乐曲
被寒冷抑制的寂静天空,恍然
复活了似曾相识的热烈而多情

抖落一身白霜的河边柳叶
也在阳光下闪动绿色
向河中的鱼儿传播着
寻亲、播种的信息
蠢蠢欲动的飞蛾,悄然宣布
四季轮回,隆重开幕
空气吹过暖暖的暗号
提醒世人
溜走的每一个时辰
活力无限,貌美年轻

Spring Is Approaching

The drizzling rain

Washed away the bitterness of winter.

Quietly

On the floating willows

Green buds grow

And yellow pedals sprout.

Soft and charming

Like the shy halo of a young girl.

The wind and the sunset are enchanted,

So are the magnolia trees downstairs.

They are so enchanted that with their hairy buds,

They become charming and elegant.

Spring is approaching.

Having gone through the summer heat,

Harvested the autumn fruits,

Stored up the winter energy.

In the warmth of your eyes,

The sky is full of fragrance.

春，来了

淅沥的小雨
洗去了冬季的苦涩
悄悄地
飘逸的柳条上
长出了绿芽
冒出了鹅黄
柔媚的
似少女泛起的羞晕
风醉了，夕阳醉了
楼下的玉兰树也醉了
醉得从毛茸茸的花苞里
长出了妩媚与淡雅
春，来了
历经了夏的酷暑
收获了秋的丰硕
积蓄着冬的能量
在你温情的回眸中
漾起满天缕缕清香

Late Autumn

It is another season of soughing autumn wind,
The golden yellow leaves fall all over the ground
As if in the blink of an eye.
Autumn has come for a long time.
There has been no free time to rest
Occasionally when I have leisure time,
I take just a few fleeting glances.
Time elapses freely between my eyes,
As if all the emotions
Have nothing to do with me.

At my middle age,
It is just like the change of seasons.
Many memories have faded away,
Youth, time, life,
Always move back and forth
In the depths of my mind.
Now I wish I could stay at the Arcadia in autumn,
To let my heart be quiet

深 秋

又一个秋风萧瑟的季节
满地飘落的金黄
仿若一眨眼
秋已来了很久
一直没有空闲休息
偶尔闲时
也是那么匆匆几眼
光阴在我的眼眸间任意流窜
仿佛一切的情感
都与我无缘

人到了中年
犹如季节到了交替的关口
很多记忆已经渐渐远去
青春流年时光
总在自己的脑海深处
来来回回地涌动
我多想停留于秋的世外
让繁杂的心得以清静

And to let my heart full of love be released.
The flowers used to be so beautiful,
The fallen flowers and leaves in front of me
Make an inexplicable feeling of longing surge.

Life will eventually go with the times,
Time will eventually take away
All the regrets.
Searching for the memories of the past,
Blurring the beautiful time,
Just like the fallen leaves on the ground at this moment,
Which can no longer return to their own branches.
Teenager, youth, middle age
Are all part of the cycle of time,
But what I worship in my heart is always
Having dreams
And Aiming high.

让满怀的情得以放逐
曾经繁花似锦
眼前残花落叶
莫名的眷恋油然而生

人生终究要与时代同行
时间也终会带走
所有的遗憾
寻找往昔的记忆
模糊了美好的光阴
就像此刻满地的落叶
再也无法回到自己的树枝
少年青年中年
都是时间周而复始的轮回
而我心中膜拜的永远是
胸怀梦想
志存高远

Night in Late Autumn

The night is frozen by the sound of dripping rain,
Fine lines of water drifting down in a dense manner.
The stars are deeply buried,
The lonely streetlights are engulfed by the mist.
The cars coming and going look as if they are suffering from melancholy:
They are manic and restless, cruelly
Knocking off the leaves of the street trees on both sides of the road.

The wind with a bitter chill
Penetrates the skin in every way,
Until it reaches the bone marrow and soul.
The alarm clock at the bedside ticks,
Knocking at the silence of the night in solitude,
Trying to print
All the noisy and painful words.

深秋的夜

夜被滴滴答答的雨声凝固
细细的水线密密麻麻飘落
星星被深深掩埋
孤寂的路灯被扫进迷雾
来往的车辆仿佛患了忧郁症——
狂躁不安,残忍地
将马路两旁的行道树叶打落

风夹着苦涩的阴冷
无孔不入地渗透进肌肤
直至骨髓和灵魂
床头的闹钟嘀嗒嘀嗒
孤独地敲着夜的寂静
试图打印
所有嘈杂而疼痛的文字

How I wish that life was like a pendulum,
Which is simple and sober,
To record the time and remember the journey,
Or I wish to forget worries and bitterness
And sleep in peace,
Dreaming happy dreams
Under the protection of thick curtains.

The leaves are tired of life,
Wailing helplessly on the ground.
The cold wind blows away the cold rain,
The moon attempts to penetrate the mists.
Vendor's hawking and a bird's chirping
Send away the darkness, the ethereal, the cold,
Waking the eyes of the sun.

多么希望像钟摆一样
简单而又清醒
记录下时间,回忆着行程
或者,忘掉烦恼和苦涩
在密实的窗帘保护下
踏实地睡眠
做一个开心的梦

树叶已经倦于生活
无奈地在地上哀鸣
冷风吹走了冷冷的雨
月亮企图穿越薄雾
一声声叫卖,一声声鸟鸣
送走了黑暗、空灵、寒冷
叫醒了太阳的眼睛

The Autumn Color

It is like a golden blanket,

Spreading over the wide field,

Connected to the distant horizon.

By day, it is as transparent as crystal,

At dusk, the afterglow is as brilliant as fire.

The clouds hang in the sky, white and crisp.

The breeze is gentle and cool.

A dry face needs a little moisturizer,

Fingernails cannot plant seeds.

The man works with the hope of harvest.

The dazzling sun shines like a knife,

The white gets bright, the yellow becomes gold.

The sickle in his hand dances with the crop,

The sweat on his forehead laughs with the fruits.

The man leads the oxen, bending down with his head held high,

秋　色

像一张金黄的毯子
铺展于宽阔的田野
连接着遥远的地平线
白昼,水晶一样透明
黄昏,余晖灿烂似火

云朵挂天,洁白爽朗
微风吹过,和煦透凉
干涩的脸上需要抹点润肤霜
指甲无法种下种子
汉子劳作着收获的希望
刺眼如刀的阳光照耀下
白的更白,黄的更黄

手中的镰,陪着庄稼舞蹈
额头的汗,伴着果子欢笑
人牵牛,昂着头弯下了腰

The oxen plowing the fields, bowing their backs and
  lowering their heads.
Shouts and prayers,
The past that cannot be forgotten can be collected.
The hatred in the heart should be forgotten.

After busy days, the snow and ice will come,
The dried up well water, the pearl of sorrow and patience,
The curve of a flock of white egrets surging up the azure
  sky.
If the autumn color enriches your eyes,
With sincerity, you should leave pure and warm blueness.

牛耕田，躬着背低下了头
一声声吆喝，一声声祈祷
无法翻卷的过往，可以收藏
心中曾经的记恨，应该遗忘

忙碌过后，冰雪即将来到
干涸的井水，心里悲忍的珍珠
一行白鹭上青天的弧度
如果，秋色丰富了你的眼睛
就用真诚，留下纯净温暖的蔚蓝

Sense of Autumn

Falling leaves raise a trace of dust,

Golden blessing:

May the fragrant soil sincerely accepts it.

May the remaining life

Bask in the sunshine and kiss the dew.

The fruit squeezes off the wilted flowers,

Glossy and shiny, you are lyrical:

O, autumn wind, please wait a moment,

I want to sing the song of harvest

To welcome the early winter morning.

The jumping and falling raindrops

Take up the responsibility of accompaniment,

Playing the romantic music.

The birds sing with a good voice,

Sending off the flying geese.

秋　意

落叶扬起一丝尘埃
金黄金黄地祈福——
芬芳的泥土真诚地接纳
让落幕的余生
沐浴阳光 亲吻露珠

果子挤落枯萎的残花
油亮油亮地抒情——
秋风啊请你等一等
我要用丰收的歌声
迎接初冬的早晨

蹦蹦跳跳飘落的雨点
承担起伴奏的责任
吹弹着浪漫的乐曲
鸟儿亮着一副好嗓门
送别雁飞的身影

The crops are transformed

A fashion is replaced by an old style.

The old buffaloes bow and march forward,

Reading the coming spring.

The partners count the harvest happily.

In the sky after the high fever,

The breeze blows off the weary look.

On the transparent face,

Fresh and crisp,

White clouds hang.

The land that has been baked all summer

Is busy trying new costume.

Youthfulness becomes maturity,

Beautiful and handsome,

Dressed in the dress of joy.

At the golden hour

The poet has more feelings that can be expressed.

Basket after basket of voices,

Singing and chanting noisily

Being full of warmth.

庄稼华丽转身
古板替代时新
老牛躬身昂扬前行
翻阅着来年的春
伙伴们欢快地数着收成

高烧过后的天空
清风悠然地吹掉倦容
通彻透明的脸上
清清爽爽
挂着一片片洁白的祥云

炙烤一夏的土地
忙碌着换装试身
青涩变成了成熟
靓丽帅气
披上了喜悦的衣裙

金色的时辰
诗人情怀抒不尽
一筐一筐的声音
喧闹地放歌欢吟
荡漾着满满的温馨

Autumn Song

Autumn breeze with coolness begins to tremble,

Falling leaves belong to the dust of the earth.

The frogs of summer are gone,

The osmanthus breathes out its last fragrance.

The willow trees by the river are thinning,

The chairs on the riverbank are moaning in solitude.

The warmth of the past is far away,

The sparkling light of the waves captures the lonely shadow on the bridge.

The nesting birds count the frosted fruits,

The plow and harrow stir the hardships of the autumn harvest.

The marks of the geese flying south are scattered,

The cold crashes into his own forehead.

A season marks an annual ring,

The earth and sky are moistened by full emotions.

The younger brother of autumn comes,

The spring brother dresses up his mood.

秋　歌

秋风带着凉意开始颤抖
落叶归属于泥土的尘埃
夏日的蛙声走了
桂花完成了最后的芳香

河边的柳树清瘦了
河岸的椅子在孤独地呻吟
昔日的温暖远了
粼粼的波光拍摄着桥上的孤影

归巢的鸟儿数着霜打的果子
犁耙搅拌着秋收的艰辛
大雁南飞的印痕散了
寒冷撞上了他自己的脑门

一个季节滚动着一个年轮
满满的情怀沁润着大地和天空
秋季的弟弟来了
春哥装扮着自己的心情

The Autumn Wind Brings Mid-Autumn

The autumn breeze sweeps across the cheeks in smile,
With a faint trace of coolness,
Freezes the breath of summer,
It blows down the yellow flowers that are getting thinner.
Leaves flutter restlessly,
And fall mercilessly even without wind.
The weeds by the roadside sway sadly,
And are full of sadness even without rain.

The autumn wind brings mid—autumn,
Frost and snow are waiting at the station ahead.
The sky has the marks of geese flying,
A poetic line of parting is drawn.
Care is ever—changing and everlasting,
The old wine is strong and weak alternatively.
Like the passing of time, old dreams are hard to remain;
Like the distant hometown, waiting with love.

秋风吹来了中秋

秋风微笑着拂过脸颊
带着一丝淡淡的凉意
凝固了夏日的气息
吹落了渐瘦的黄花
树叶不安分地纷纷扬扬
没有风也无情落下
路边野草凄美摇曳
没有雨也愁绪满怀

秋风吹来了中秋
霜雪在前方的驿站等待
天空留下雁飞的印痕
划出一道离别的诗行
圆了会缺缺了会圆的牵挂
浓了会淡淡了会浓的陈酒
像是流逝的光阴,旧梦难留
像是遥远的故乡,痴情守候

I can read your mood,

You also understand my nostalgia.

We are looking at each other across the starry river,

Waiting for Wu Gang,

Waiting for the wine brewed from osmanthus.

For so many years, so many generations,

The same story has been told again and again.

The same moonlight we have been waiting for again and again,

Autumn wind! It's the autumn wind that brings mid-autumn.

我能读懂你的意境

你也明白我的乡愁

我们在星河两岸遥望

等待着吴刚

等待着桂花酿的酒

多少年啊多少代

同一个故事讲了又讲

同一个月色盼了又盼

秋风啊！是秋风吹来了中秋

New Year's Eve

Again at the end of the year, the streets are full of
The rich taste of home: sausages, rice dumpling leaves.
Frozen meat hide in the corner of the kitchen,
Accompanied by the fragrance of dried vegetables in the
 house.

Migrant workers catch the last train home,
Evacuating the last line of defense of the winter.
Construction sites became isolated islands,
The silence, a moment of nowhere to be found.

In the dark and mysterious underground cave,
Tree roots and shelled seeds
And water infiltrated, covered with straw bales.
Stirring, like a cry for survival.

The rich has nothing to do with the cold, not wasting
 meat and wine.
A few firework rockets rush out of the night, lighting up

年 关

又一个岁末年关,满街飘过
浓郁的家乡味道:腊肠,粽叶
鳌冻肉躲在厨房的角落里
陪伴着乌干菜满屋飘香

民工赶上回家的末班车
撤离这冬日的最后防线
工地,成了一座孤岛
寂静,无处可寻的时刻

黑暗神秘的地下洞窟中
树根和带壳的种子
和水的渗透,草包覆盖
骚动,像是为生存的呐喊

朱门与寒冷无关,酒肉未臭
夜色里冲出几只窜天猴,点亮

The dazzling scenes which change and transform.

A pair of couplets refresh the facade of our own homes.

Take off the business and fatigue from the body,

With laughter and wine, the songs of the Chinese New Year are sung.

The sunset embraces the smiling snowman,

Hoping for the eternal recovery of all things.

耀眼的景物更替变换
一副对联,刷新了自家门面

脱下身上的忙碌和疲惫
笑语与浊酒寒暄着新春的歌吟
夕阳拥抱着笑容可掬的雪人
企盼着万物复苏的永恒

Winter Morning

Sunlight and white frost intertwine

Like a gentle knife,

Stab awake the winter morning.

The charming fish are still sleeping peacefully,

The diligent birds are singing the morning song,

Urging the beautiful fish to wake up quickly.

Come on! As the morning star of the south,

Hurry to meet the goddess of the sunset in the south of
   Yangtze River,

Leaving the drunkenness of last night in your memory.

If the darkness of the sky is used again

To cover the moon that lights up the earth at night,

How boring it would be!

Look at the light outside the window, how dazzling it is!

The cloudless sky is like a velvet blanket,

Softly spreading over the fields.

Only the dark shadows made by the tall buildings

冬之晨

阳光和白霜交织
像一把温柔的刀
刺醒了冬日的早晨
妩媚的鱼儿,还在安眠
勤快的小鸟,吹响了晨曲
催促美鱼儿,快快醒来

来吧!作为南方的晨星
赶紧来会见江南朝霞的女神
将昨夜的醉意留在记忆里
如果再用天空那一层幽暗
遮住夜晚点亮大地的月亮
那样是多么的无聊
看看窗外的光芒,耀眼无比

蔚蓝色的天空,像绒毯
柔柔地铺展于田野
只有被高楼照下的暗影

And the white frost on the vegetables and crops,
Make the green fresher and more tender.
The creek that has slept all night
Makes the sound of gurgling water brighter.

The house glowed with amber light,
Floor heating is mixed with sunshine, making the furniture
Crackle pleasantly.
Fried eggs, milk, and bread are fragrant.
However, should put your means of transportation
Into operation as soon as possible?

Go downstairs with clothes on, enduring the hardships of a
　long journey.
Slip past the early morning greeting,
Street trees running backwards.
Bamboo forests sway in the distance,
The people in front of me are in a hurry.
No wind whistling the cold of winter,
No frozen thoughts,
There is only the warm rhythm of light, fresh and lovable.

还有打过蔬菜和庄稼的白霜
浸润着绿色更加鲜嫩
熟睡一夜的小河
发出愈加晶亮的潺潺水声

屋里泛着琥珀的光辉
地暖和着阳光,家具
发出愉快的噼啪响声
牛奶面包煎鸡蛋,香气扑鼻
然而,你是否应该及早
把代步工具送上机械的暖风

披衣下楼,一路风尘
滑过清晨的问候
行道树向后奔跑
远处竹林摇曳
眼前身影匆匆
没有风的呼啸冬的寒冷
没有冻僵的思绪
只有暖暖的光韵,清新可亲

Snowy Night

Snow

Is a falling leave from the sky,

Sleeping on the trees on earth.

I

Did something heavenly

On the ground.

Tick tock tick tock,

Which is the snore of snow melting

And the echo of my sighs.

雪 夜

雪
天空的落叶
睡在人间的树上

我
在地面上
做了些天上的事

滴答滴答
是雪化的鼾呼
也是我唏嘘的回音

Rainy Night in Early Winter

The rain in early winter is softly

Dripping all night long

To announce to the world

A cold winter

is coming quietly.

Then you can use

The silence of the night,

Prepare warm attire

To keep your eyes open

Until the gentle dawn comes.

Let me try tonight

Hover at the door of dreams

Challenge the sleepy eyes

To stop me from sleeping in peace,

Waiting for heaven's handouts.

Darkness is the battery of man

初冬的雨夜

初冬的雨柔韧地
滴滴答答整夜不眠
向世人告示着
一个寒冷的冬天
正在悄悄地走来

那你就可以用
黑夜的沉默
准备取暖的装束
让你的眼睛睁开
直到温柔的黎明来临

今晚就让我尝试
在梦的门前徘徊
挑战瞌睡的双眼
不让自己安眠
等待着上天的施舍

黑夜是人的蓄电池

Early winter is the best energy storage time.
Prepare for the journey of the year,
Accept the invitation of life with grace,
Experience darkness and light.

I want to set out in this sacred night
Listening to the sound of all the noise and glory.
With the sky, the earth and the life
Wrapped in the rainy night of early winter,
To meet all the wind and cold.

The passing of life tells me
The day is to make a living
And the night is for love.
People often go to bed early,
Only the lovers whisper to the heart all night long.

Do you hear it? There is a voice
Calling to you in the silence of the night.
Asking you to wake up in this precious hour,
Forget your body and integrate into it,
Witnessing together every aspect of life.

初冬正是最佳的蓄能时刻
准备着一年的旅程
从容接受生活的邀请
体验黑暗与光明

我要在这个神圣的夜晚出发
听着一切嘈杂和荣耀的声音
与天与地与生活的自己
裹挟着初冬的雨夜
迎接一切的风和冷

生活的过往告诉我
白天是为了谋生
而黑夜才是为了情怀
常人往往早早入睡
只有爱者整夜向心灵低语

听见了吗？有一个声音
在寂静的夜里呼唤着你
要你在这珍贵的时分,醒来
忘却自己的身体,融入其中
共同见证生命的点滴

Looking Up at the Starry Sky

The title is indeed a bit old—fashioned,
But why it's still seductive?
Writers are writing about it, and painters are painting about it,
Children and the old are looking up to it.
The starry sky that changes every moment
Carries your hopes and my dreams.

Tonight starry sky is not as empty as last night,
Tonight, the moon needs to go in a bigger direction,
I'm looking for from among the stars
The brightest one, which should belong to me.

In the fresh breeze, the willow leaves by the river are cutting the water.
I stand on this side of the bridge,
Chanting the poems in my heart.
Looking up at myself and the starry sky,
I feel as profound as God.

仰望星空

这个题目确实有点陈旧
为何依然充满诱惑力
文人在写，画家在画
孩子和老人都在仰望
每时每刻都在变幻的星空
载着你的希翼，我的梦想

今夜的星空不是昨夜那么空
今夜的月亮需要往大的方向
繁星点点，我在寻找
最闪亮的那一颗，应该属于我

微风清逸，河边柳条划开水面
我站在桥的这一边
吟诵着心中的诗句
仰望自己和星空
就像上帝一样深长

I hear the echoes from beyond the sky,
Whoever can move the Big Dipper
Can remove the bright light.

I am silent, then I speak smilingly.
The brightness of the stars belongs only to the red carpet,
I simply want the light that belongs to me.
Is it that God does not understand me, or that I do not understand God?
My looking up is a kind of attachment, a kind of expectation,
And a kind of yearning of the earth.

我听见天外发来的回声
谁能将北斗星搬动
谁就能移走璀璨光芒

我沉默,然后我笑言
星光的璀璨只属于红毯
我只要属于我的那一束光
是上帝不懂我,还是我不懂上帝
我的仰望是一种牵挂,一种期盼
一种大地的向往

Best Time in Life

The years quietly flow forward
We need to move forward after all.
Don't hesitate,
There is no need to be indecisive.
A turn
Can't take away the hardships of the journey.
One glance back
Can't tolerate the sadness of life.

A life
Is simply a journey
I don't know where it started,
It's hard to track.
In the corners of time,
It's hard to avoid stumbles.
All the excitement
Is after all, just a passing fog.

人生好时光

岁月静静向前流淌
我们终究需要前行
不要犹豫
不必彷徨
一个转身
带不走跋涉的坎坷
一眼回眸
无法包容生活的悲凉

人生
仅仅是一段旅程
不知起点
难觅踪影
光阴的转角里
难免磕磕碰碰
一切的轰轰烈烈
毕竟都是过眼烟云

All the stories

Will be yellowed on the paper of memory.

I am chanting a verselet,

Not to exaggerate my feelings;

I write about longing,

Not to remember the past.

The road is under my feet,

My heart is on the road.

In the notes of life,

There is never a repetition of a chapter.

When the black hair turns grey,

When I look back suddenly,

The warmth is still in my heart,

That is a best time of life.

所有的故事
都会在记忆的素笺上泛黄
我吟小诗
不为渲染心事
我书眷恋
不为记住曾经的过往

路在脚下
心在路上
生命的音符里
从来没有重复的篇章
待到青丝缀满霜华
蓦然回首
暖意依然满怀
便是人生好时光

This Night Is So Bustling

The sound of motor breaks the silence of the night,
A few young people's roses and sunshine
Enliven the quiet residential quarter.
Jinmao, my neighbor Zhang's dog
Has started a choir of barks with others.
This night is so noisy.

The noise has brought heat and dust,
Rendering the starlight and the night wind no longer warm.
Cicadas have climbed the trees and started to roar,
And the frogs have begun to shout.
This night is so noisy.

A black forest
Is separated by a silvery white band.
Shimmering scattered fragments shatter
Between the branches of the roadside trees.
A few shades of light swing through the window,

这个晚上真吵

马达声打破了夜的寂静
几个年轻人的玫瑰和阳光
沸腾了小区的宁静
隔壁老张家的金毛
带着狗狗们一起合唱
这个晚上真吵

嘈杂声吹来了暑热与风尘
星光和夜风不再温情
知了爬在树上开始咆哮
蛙声也变成了呐喊
这个晚上真吵

一片黑色森林
流泻一带银白
行道树枝间
散落一地闪烁的碎片
窗口摇进几点光影

Lightning and thunder in my heart roaring,
This night is so noisy.

I wonder where you are tonight.
In this noisy night,
Are you also hiding from the diseases and moans of the earth,
And refusing to become old and retarded?
Are you quietly swallowing the mercury of moonlight
In the midst of the rivalry between quietness and noise?

心目中的闪电和雷声齐鸣
这个晚上真吵

不知今晚你在哪里
是否也在这个吵闹的晚上
躲避大地上的疾病和呻吟
也在拒绝苍老和迟钝
在安静与嘈杂的对擂中
静静吞食月光的水银

Smile, Like the Blooming and Heading of the Grain

Heaven always arranges surprises for us,

Sometimes making our eyes overflow with tears,

Sometimes making the mind step into the landscape gallery.

At this time we are like a rice plant,

Smiles are the wheat ears growing from the leaves,

Can lead to rainy and windy autumn scenery,

And bring out the whispers from the nestling ones.

In the warmth and humidity of human society,

What cannot be crushed or blown away are

Smiles, the small flowers blooming from the branches of the time

Can prove that the bloom belongs to the fruit.

Love the rice that has been immersed in water,

Like loving us who seem to grow in the water.

Love the love smiles produced,

Starting from the bottom of heart,

Bloom and head sprouting in a lifetime.

微笑,像禾谷的扬花抽穗

上天总会给我们安排惊喜
有时会让眼睛溢出泪花
有时会让心境步入山水画廊
此时我们像一株水稻
微笑就是叶鞘中长出的麦穗
可以荡漾出风雨秋色
可以冉冉飘起相偎相依的私语

在红尘的温暖和潮湿里
碾不碎也吹不散的是
微笑,岁月枝头下绽放的小花
来证明绽放是属于果实的

热爱一直浸在水中的水稻
就像热爱仿佛在水中成长的我们
热爱微笑出的缱绻
从心囊出发
一世一生地扬花抽穗

A Farewell to Brussels

From the far East,
I came to the "dwelling on the swamp".
Long sigh like a female swordplayer in Peking Opera:
A god in front of me,
A goddess behind me,
Led me through the gate of UBI.

With the sky as the base and the cloud as the color,
The Grand—Place
Dyes the medieval civilization blue.
The Renaissance was still in a hurry,
The naked Manneken Pis had not yet grown up,
The burning fuse was still placed at the crossroads of Europe.
"A specter of communism"
Wandered here and spread over the world gredually.

St. Michael's Cathedral
Are many smiling faces under the doctoral mortarboards.

再见！布鲁塞尔

我从遥远的东方
来到"沼泽上的住所"
像刀马旦一声长叹
前面一个男神
后面一个女神
引我进入 UBI 的大门

天为胎云为色
布鲁塞尔广场
染蓝了中世纪的文明
文艺复兴还在匆匆路上
光着身子的小于连还没有长大
燃烧的导火索还放在欧洲的十字路口
"一个共产主义的幽灵"
从这里徘徊出韵脚

圣米歇尔大教堂
是博士帽下的一张张笑脸

The skies of Europe. I look up to it,
With my right hand on my chest
Trying to hear my heart beating.

I was not alone in visiting this land,
I was not alone in appreciating the clean Senna River.
Visiting them on behalf of my motherland,
Three days, how long they were!
It was a long time to see a country like a square.

A flock of white doves flew up,
It was as if I had become a little bird too.
In the Belgian capital. At NATO headquarters,
In the political heart of Europe, I flew
With the wind, with the clouds, with freedom.

I flew back again. I must come back.
I couldn't pass through the downtown,
The moaning and shouting of refugees
Stung my ears.
I couldn't fly over the sea,
The floating bodies of those who drowned fleeing the war
Stung my eyes.

欧洲的天空 我仰视着
右手放在胸口
想听到传到我内心的跳动

不是一个人踏上了这片土地
不是一个人领略谐纳河的清澈
以祖国的方式参访
三天,多么漫长
漫长出一个国度像一座广场

一群白鸽飞起
我仿佛也成了一只小鸟
在比利时首都。在北约总部
在欧洲政治集中地,飞翔
随风,随云,随自由

我又飞了回来。必须回来
不能途经闹市
难民的呻吟和呐喊
刺伤了耳朵
不能在大海上空飞翔
那漂浮着为逃避战火而溺亡的尸体
刺痛了眼睛

I couldn't stay where there's air,

The smell of gunpowder after a horrible explosion

Made me lose the sense of smell.

I suddenly felt

This wooden country of freedom and civilization

Is like a journey through the past: brittle and fragile,

Even easily spontaneous combustion into ashes and no longer remembered

Goodbye! Laconian Castle

The light of the crown leaked

And shined on your subjects.

The yearning and worship in my heart

Remained in the land where the Five-Star Red Flag flies.

I had to go back to tour my blacked-topped boat,

You could only leave me a short memory.

And in my motherland on the water,

I have a bedroom in the river:

Light, Elegant.

Alone or with others,

Or quiet or mighty.

不能在有空气的地方停留
恐怖爆炸后浓浓的火药味
让嗅觉失灵
我突然觉得
这木质的自由文明的国度
像旅途中的过往：易脆易碎
甚至易自燃成灰烬而不再记得

再见！拉肯城堡
王冠的光芒漏下来
普照你的臣民吧
我心中的向往和膜拜
还在飘扬着五星红旗的土地
我要回去游一游我的乌篷船
你只能留给我短暂的记忆
而在我水中的祖国
我拥有水上的卧室
轻快。闲雅
或独或群
或清清静静
或浩浩荡荡

You Are My Window

You are my window, accompanying
The gentle wakeup in the morning.
Receiving the greeting of spring and the smile of winter.
As if it's the ignorant teenager, or
It's the time of budding youth,
The first shining light in the sky
Only accepts the window's worship.

You are my window, the light
Cover stars, shines on
Full memories, exquisite and clear.
My heart flies comfortably
And is seemingly unable to see myself.
Toward the horizon,
I don't know where the night settles.

You are my window, on all sides
The sky is clear and blue; there is hustle and bustle in the city.

你是我的窗

你是我的窗,陪伴
清晨那般温柔的醒来
接受春的问候冬的微笑
仿佛是懵懂的少年,抑或
青春萌动的时节
那天上的第一束闪亮
只许接受窗的膜拜

你是我的窗,光芒
镶满了星星,照耀
满满的回忆,玲珑剔透
我的心惬意地飘翔着
似乎看不到自己
朝着地平线的方向
不知夜色在哪里落脚

你是我的窗,四面
净蓝的天空,都市喧嚣

I am still me as if I were in a land of Cockaigne,

I am in the middle of the infinite world.

I see nothing but the green that I love,

Quiet, beautiful, fragrant.

Don't let anyone hear,

Don't be disturbed,

Take me to dreams leisurely.

依然是我,宛若世外
置身于无限的大千之中
满眼倾心相爱的绿色
幽静、美艳、芬芳
不要有人听见
不要有人打扰
悠然地带我入梦乡

The Bright Red Flag

After expecting for ten months,
One is born.
The life of every Chinese person
is engraved with a red mark.
The first colorful memory developed after opening eyes
is the bright red flag.

In July 1921,
Thirteen foresighted intellectuals
With the ideal of saving the country
Walked into a house on Huangpi Road in Shanghai.
They burned with passion,
Raising the glaring red faith
On the boat in the South Lake.

The bright red flag,
Why are you so bright?
Because it's colored by the blood of countless martyrs
In the pursuit of truth.

鲜红的旗帜

十月怀胎
呱呱坠地
每一个中国人的生命里
都刻上了红色印记
睁开眼睛的第一次彩色记忆
就是鲜红的旗帜

一九二一年七月
十三名先知先觉的知识分子
怀着救国的理想
走进上海黄陂路的小屋里
他们激情燃烧
将红色的信仰
在南湖的船上耀眼升起

鲜红的旗帜啊
为什么鲜艳无比
因为那是无数先烈
追求真理留下的血迹

From the moment of its birth,
The Party has taken national development as its mission.
The workers and peasants carried the bright red flag
To lead the Chinese Revolution to victory.

March northward, march northward.
The Party led the Red Army soldiers
In climbing snow-capped mountains,
And moving across muddy grasslands,
Travelling 25,000 li with great hardship.
The old squad leader and the young Red Army kid fell
With the red flags in their hands standing firm.

Resist Japanese aggression, resist Japanese aggression,
In the grave crisis between life and death,
The Party took up the national mission.
The blood of the anti-Japanese generals and soldiers
Colored you red.
General Jingyu swallowed cotton to keep fighting,
Shot his last bullet
With the bright red flag still standing majestically.

从诞生那一刻起

就以天下为己任

工农盟友扛着鲜红的旗帜

推动中国革命取得胜利

北上,北上

引领着红军战士

翻过茫茫雪山

走过泥泞草地

艰苦跋涉两万五千里

老班长红小鬼倒下了

手中的红旗巍然而立

抗日,抗日

在生死存亡的危急关头

担负起民族大义

抗日将士的鲜血

红透了你

靖宇将军吞棉而战

打光最后一粒子弹

鲜红的旗仍然屹立

From northeast China

To the banks of the Yellow River,

From the Taihang Mountains

To the southern battlefields,

Where there was battle

There were bright red flags.

The darkness of the Zhazidong Prison

Couldn't block your light.

Fingers pierced by bamboo sticks

And the needles and threads dipped in blood

Embroidered the red flag.

Ninety—seven years have passed.

The bright red flag,

From the groundbreaking of the First National Party Congress

To the Zunyi Meeting at the critical moment between life and death,

From the Long March to the north to resist against Japanese aggression,

To the decisive liberation of the whole China,

从白山黑水

到黄河岸边

从太行山上

到南方战场

哪里有战斗

哪里就有鲜红的旗帜

渣滓洞的黑暗

没能挡住你的光明

被竹签刺破的手指

蘸着血迹的针线

绣出红彤彤的旗

九十七年了

鲜红的旗帜啊

从中共一大的开天辟地

到生死关头的遵义会议

从万里长征北上抗日

到摧枯拉朽解放全中国

From the raising of the Five—Star Red Flag in front of
 Tiananmen Gate
To the bright future of national rejuvenation.
Nineteen important congresses
Were recorded in the history of the Party splendidly.
One step left one resounding footprint.
The bright red flag
Flutters high in the motherland.

从天安门前升起五星红旗
到民族复兴迎来光明前景
十九次重要的会议
彪炳于党的史册
一步一个铿锵的足迹
鲜红的旗帜啊
高高飘扬在祖国大地

Herpes' Pain

Who was it? Who was so cruel that pricks like a needle
From the skin into the flesh deep.
Herpes, a virus that attacked my body,
Destroying the peripheral nerves of the muscles,
Causing the stinging pain night after night, day after day
Pushing the limits of sleepless nights.

Like a kelp wrapped around the chest,
It was hard to bear, the barbs were wrapped with countless
    bacteria,
Flooding me with annoying blisters.
Tormenting me and sucking the spirit from my body.
The ointment was applied over and over, layer after layer.
A long, slow, torturous process of recovery was tormenting,
Testing my patience and perseverance.

I prayed for my body to heal over as soon as possible,
Time and time again I stepped through the hospital doors.
But the night was so quiet.

疱疹之痛

是谁？是谁这般狠毒，针刺
从肌肤钻进皮肉深处
疱疹，是病毒侵袭了身体
破坏了肌肉末梢神经
让刺痛夜复一夜，日复一日
挑战着夜不能眠的极限

像一条海带缠在了胸口
难忍，倒刺裹挟着无数细菌
恣意泛滥着恼人的水泡
折磨你，并吸走人体的精神
药抹了一遍又一遍一层又一层
一段漫长的修复过程，煎熬
考验着人的耐心和毅力

我祈祷着肌体尽快平复
一次次踏进医院的大门
夜却如此寂静

I dreamt that the pain would quietly go away
And healthy cells would defeat the invasion of bacteria,
Resisting against all the reactionary vermin.

I would overcome the disease with my will.
If I finally won one day,
Giving me back a healthy body of life.
I would cry splendidly,
Weeping for an excruciating pain at the dead of night,
Clenching my fist to silently fight against the darkness.

梦想着疼痛会悄悄远离
健康细胞打败细菌的入侵
抵抗一切反动的害人精

我要用意志战胜病魔
如果终于有一天胜利了
重新赐予我健康的生命之躯
我就会灿烂地哭泣
哭泣自己在钻心之痛的黑夜
攥紧拳头默默地与黑暗抗争

Don't Crush My Dream

Who can crush my dream with sound?
Maybe only this annoying pile driver.
The noise of every pounding
Crushes my dream like a mortar.
This pile of steel supports churning with mud,
Is as cold as ice, with a grudge against dreams.

Neighbors flee from their dreams for a few minutes,
The whole neighborhood has woken up from their dreams.
Children cover their ears,
A few middle-aged or old men raise their voices.
Cursing and the noise of pile driving hit the night sky.
Piling is for the foundation of urban construction,
This pile driver, however, seems to be a psychopath,
Howling loudly in the face of the land, lacking power,
Tonight, it's absolutely necessary to use the foundation to oppose the dream.

别碾碎我的梦境

谁能用声音来碾压我的梦境
或许只有这台讨厌的桩机
每一次撞击的声音
像迫击炮一般,击碎我的梦
这堆搅和着烂泥的钢铁支架
冷若冰霜,与梦有仇

邻居们从梦境中逃出,几分钟
整个小区都已经梦醒
小孩们捂住自己的耳朵
几个中年或者老人扯开了嗓门
咒骂,与桩击的噪声冲击着夜空
打桩,是为城市建设夯实基础
这台桩机,却似精神病患者
面对土地大声嚎叫,缺乏力量
今晚,绝然要用基础对立梦想

The night is to nurture the peace of dreams,

Operator, you don't know the rules of the city.

Your rough-and-rendy or and even savagery

Attempt to torture the city into melancholy.

This ancient city is already more than 2,000 years old,

Spring, summer, autumn and winter are embedded in it,

Still carries the responsibility of nurturing.

You use a deafening dark night,

To disturb the sleep of the city's elderly city,

And crush the peace that belongs to the night.

You have evil intentions. How should you be punished for that?

夜,是为了孕育梦境的安宁
操作工,你不懂城里的规矩
你的粗暴甚至野蛮
企图把城市折磨成忧郁症
这座古城,已经两千多岁
春夏秋冬嵌于其中
依然承载着养育的责任
你用一个震耳欲聋的黑夜
搅乱城市老人的睡眠
碾碎属于夜色的宁静
你居心叵测,该当何罪

Delaying

The hall at the security checkpoint

Was crowded, without a single cranny, like a barrier lake.

Shouting, roaring, accusing,

And shouting abuse at the cries of children

Overwhelmed one after another,

Drowning out the roar of the engines.

Countless middle—aged or elderly people

Raised their hands above their heads,

Falling down,

and then standing up.

Like broken lotus roots,

Attempting to break through the congested mouth of the lake.

The arrival entrance was so quiet that

You can count the sound of footsteps.

The greeters stood in a line,

Without joy and without inquiries.

A few scattered pieces of luggage

延　误

安检口的大厅
像个堰塞湖
拥挤,没有一丝空隙
呼声吼声指责声
谩骂着小孩的哭声
一声高过一声
淹没了引擎的轰鸣
无数个中年或是老人
双手举过头顶
像残缺的断藕
一会儿倒下
一会儿立起
企图砸开拥堵的湖口

到达口很静
可以数清脚步的声音
迎客的站成一排
没有喜悦,没有问询
几件稀稀拉拉的行李

On the conveyor belt,

Received a mechanized inspection.

The staff in uniform

Looked at the loneliness dully,

With an expression of indifferency on their faces.

The loudspeaker was still announcing:

Sorry, so—and—so flight is cancelled.

Sorry, so—and—so flight is delayed.

The departure lobby was chaotic,

The arrival hall was quiet.

The departing guests were in a hurry,

Sad for the waiting relatives.

在传送带上
接受着机械化式的检阅
穿着制服的工作人员
木讷地张望着孤独
脸上挂着禁止通行的表情

广播里还在通知
对不起,某某航班取消
对不起,某某航班延误
新世纪,祖先的理念
到达大厅很静
急煞了赶路的客人
愁苦了等待的亲人

The Circulatory Wish

Time has the desire to come back,
There is the aspiration for love, attached to the spirit.
Time also has to go away once and for all, helplessly
Breaking all the passing into pieces,
Throwing it into another world.

Joy has the desire to return,
Rushing to cover the darkness in life,
Putting all the hardness on hold,
Letting you sleep soundly in the night, and then
Facing the hustle and bustle of the world.

Where does the desire unwanted come from?
Where does it end up with?
Facing loneliness, walking silently.
Four seasons circulate, only the heat and cold
Wait for a long time on the curved road.

循环的愿望

时间有要回来的愿望
有爱的初心,依附于精神
也有要一去不返,无奈地
将一切的过往打碎
扔进另一个世界

喜悦有要回来的愿望
赶来遮蔽生命中的黑暗
将一切的难,搁置
让你在夜里沉睡,然后
面对喧嚣的尘世

而不想拥有的愿望
解于谁人,落于谁心
面对孤独,默然前行
四季更替,唯有燥热和寒冷
长久等在弯曲的道路上

Perhaps, only when the drums of mourning are beaten in
 the chest,
The arms carved with justice begin to shout,
Time returns from midnight to midnight and freezes.
The back carrying the heavy universe, wish
Will no longer move a step away from this poem.

或许，只有当胸膛擂响丧鼓
刻着正义的双臂开始高呼
时间从零点回到零点，凝固
背负着沉重宇宙的脊背，愿望
不再从这首诗里移开一步

Thinking of You at the Dead of Night

Thinking of you in the dead of night.
I think of the eagle flying in the blue sky,
Thinking of the angelic white clouds.
Not just because I love them, but because I simply miss them.
It's not a debt from a past life, it's only a promise.
Though the years have passed, the memories are yellowed,
The feeling when we first met is deep-rooted in my heart.

Life is supposed to be one encounter after another,
The ones that fade into oblivion are only your transients,
Only the ones that are engraved in your mind belong to you.
At that time, the sky will grow in your heart,
Big enough for the wind and for the rain;
Big enough for the heat and for the cold;
Big enough for dreams soaring.

在夜深人静时想你

在夜深人静时想你
想翱翔蓝天的雄鹰
想天使般美丽的白云
不仅仅因为爱情，只是想念
不是前世的亏欠，只是约定
岁月流逝，虽已泛黄了记忆
初遇时的感觉，深深潜入心底

人生本来就是一次次相遇
慢慢淡忘的只是你的过客
只有刻骨铭心的才属于自己
那时的你心里会长出天空
装得下风，装得下雨
装得下酷暑，装得下寒冷
任一个个梦想翱翔驰骋

The soul has the desire to pursue an aim,

Dreams are transformed into clouds of lightness.

Through the coordinates, through time and space,

Look forward to the next happy meeting.

Choose a brand new appointment,

To complete a journey that nourishes the spirit.

心灵有了追求归宿的渴望
梦想幻化成了云淡风轻
穿过坐标,穿越时空
期待下一次幸福的相逢
选择一个崭新的约定
成全一段滋润心田的旅程

It's Dusk Again

At the sunset,

A person walks silently,

Like a bird flying across the sky,

Enchantingly beautiful.

An open and vast land,

With desolate grass.

All the sorrows and joys of life

Are hidden in the cycle of seasons.

When the beauty of the light fades away;

And can no longer be held up,

It will eventually disappear under a flush of setting sun.

Can I

Stand here

Quietly,

Watching the back of the aging time?

又是黄昏

夕阳下
一个人默默行走
倦鸟飞过天空
分外妖娆美丽
一片空旷辽阔的大地
荒草萋萋
一切生命的悲喜
都隐藏在季节的轮回里
当锦瑟的韶光渐行渐远
再也无法掬起
终究要消失在这一抹斜阳里
我是否可以
站在这里
静静地
看着时光老去的背影

图书在版编目 (CIP) 数据

水质时光 / 虞学泽著；童孝华译. -- 北京：中央编译出版社，2023.6
　　ISBN 978-7-5117-4431-9

Ⅰ. ①水… Ⅱ. ①虞… ②童… Ⅲ. ①诗集—中国—当代 Ⅳ. ① I227

中国国家版本馆 CIP 数据核字 (2023) 第 089104 号

水质时光

责任编辑	何　蕾
插画作者	一　一
责任印制	刘　慧
出版发行	中央编译出版社
地　　址	北京市海淀区北四环西路69号（100080）
电　　话	（010）55627391（总编室）　（010）55627116（编辑室）
	（010）55627320（发行部）　（010）55627377（新技术部）
经　　销	全国新华书店
印　　刷	浙江越生联合出版印刷有限公司
开　　本	889毫米×1194毫米 1/32
字　　数	149千字
印　　张	10.125
版　　次	2023年6月第1版
印　　次	2023年6月第1次印刷
定　　价	89.00元

新浪微博：@中央编译出版社　　　微　信：中央编译出版社（ID：cctphome）
淘宝店铺：中央编译出版社直销店（http://shop108367160.taobao.com）（010）55627331

本社常年法律顾问：北京市吴栾赵阎律师事务所律师　闫军　梁勤
凡有印装质量问题，本社负责调换，电话：（010）55626985